TWISTED LIBRARY
VOLUME 1

SHORT HORROR STORIES ANTHOLOGY

BRYCE NEALHAM

MORE BOOKS FROM THIS AUTHOR

 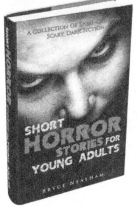 

CONTENTS

STORY 1

They Sleep At The Foot Of Our Beds

I still can't sleep, it's after midnight and there is literally someone, I feel but cannot see, lying in my bed with me and breathing heavily in my face.

The hot breath in my face is real and it smells rank like rotten eggs and blood. The blankets I am cowering under are soft and warm and I'm not dreaming. I'm wide awake and I feel sick and the fact I can feel all of my senses means I am fully alert and this is real.

I've been physically sick every single day since I lost them both and I swear this thing is slowly draining me of my life force.

I don't know what this thing is going to do to me and now that I am lying wide awake, sleep deprived and wondering how long it will take for my body to be found, all I can do is reflect on how I got here.

As long as I have been a little girl I have felt stalked by something. A man, and I don't know what he is but I sometimes wonder if he is not human. Since having cats I have felt a little safer, the man seems to be kept at bay and I can only feel his presence when I am stressed or tired.

When we sleep our guards are down, we are vulnerable to anything and we are exposed to all kinds of dangers but we don't know it.

Perhaps there may be a white tip spider crawling in our sheets waiting to bite us as we move in our sleep, perhaps we left a heater on and may be at risk of carbon monoxide poisoning? Who is to say that dangers are always those we know when there are also dangers out of this world that science cannot explain?

Sensitive types, pets and those who are close to death may feel these types of energies like us and some entities may like our energy and stalk us until we have nothing left.

I haven't felt safe since both my cats passed away, there is something currently tormenting me and I don't know what it is and what it wants. I don't think it's even human.

I used to see this figure as a little girl and it used to run at me from the corner of my eyes whenever I was focused on my schoolwork. Whenever I turned my head to look at it it would disappear in a flash but the way it had moved at me was too real.

I couldn't have been hallucinating and whenever I saw it I felt a sense of dread. I used to sleep so much better when both of my cats were living with me, but they passed away a few weeks ago and not only am I grieving them and missing them immensely but I am feeling vulnerable spiritually.

I feel suggestible to psychic attacks and now that both of my cats are gone I haven't been feeling safe happy or safe since.

My cats used to watch over me as I slept, my youngest used to always sleep by my feet, which in hindsight I learnt was a protective gesture. She slept at my feet because she was protecting me from something and now I am starting to remember what she was protecting me from.

Though she had been a tiny white and beautiful cat she felt fiercely protective of me. My eldest pure black cat only brought me joy and happiness and she used to see and react to things that I couldn't see.

They were both beautiful and very intuitive rescue cats, I saved them and they saved me.

Sometimes when we had all been cuddling together they both used to look behind me and start growling and hissing at something that had been directly behind me. Some nights my neighbors motion activated floodlight had been triggered but there was nothing in sight, yet something set off the sensor.

One day I woke to find the front window of my car smashed and I had no recollection of who would do something like that. All I had was my instinct that night that there was someone stalking me and waiting for me outside of my unit and that night my cats had been guarding me

A former partner once claimed that a spirit of a little girl was protecting me against a bad man and that had been too much of a creepy confidence for me to ignore. He'd told me he saw her hovering over me and patting my cheek softly as I peacefully slept. I've since moved on and though her spirit never followed me to my new house, the man she was trying to protect me from did.

After losing both cats I feel I can't breathe and on a good day I stumble through my day but my appreciation for life and creativity is gone and I can't face my loved ones. I had lost my eldest first and my youngest second, they weren't close but they still enjoyed each other's company enough to get on, rub noses, share food and sleep in close proximity.

All I can do now is reflect; I can't sleep or get comfortable so I am forced to reflect. I feel like a failure and I'm trying to tune out the cruel presence haunting me and I am trying to ignore its heavy breathing in my ear.

The heavy breathing is predatory, almost taunting as if he is daring me to try and fall asleep. I hug my soft pillows to my chest and heave and sob heavily, I know this thing is going to break my mind before it kills me.

I reflect on my family and friends, on my work mates who are the only ones I see now. They heard about my cats passing through my loved ones and had noticed I'd stopped smiling and laughing. Everyone noticed but no one knew how to approach me or knew what to say, they wanted to help but they knew I was broken.

My grief is the price to pay for years of happy memories and a happiness I'd never known without my cats but I can't justify why this thing is literally breathing down my neck now.

I know I'm not going to be able to sleep tonight and I wonder if I will be remembered as a good person. I haven't returned calls from family or friends and I know they have been worried about me.

I try to sense the presence of my cats but I can't feel them and I would give anything to have them cuddled up with me instead of this thing. I'm consumed by anger and grief and he's all I sense and he doesn't intend to comfort me.

I reflect on my encounters with this thing over the course of the last few days. He has been hunting me for some time and he is forcing me to accept that I am now his. He is only toying with me and I know he won't leave me alone until he has claimed me as his own.

Only hours before I had been in the shower and suddenly I got a gust of putrid breath in my face and it had come from nowhere and the smell had been rank.

Earlier this morning I took a short nap on my lounge and when I opened my eyes I had seen him standing at the top of my stairs and grinning down at me, how long he had been there for I don't want to know. I would have preferred a human stalker, one that I could deal with properly because I am not equipped to deal with this type of entity.

I need to ride this out and ignore him for as long as I can. I feel it now, he is trying to drive me to madness and he wants me to relapse.

My cats stopped me from doing stupid things, my cats gave me a purpose to live and the chance to look after them and learn how to look after myself. I need to keep looking after myself now without them and I cannot let this man (if he is even a man) hurt me.

It was like my cats were keeping him away from me, cats are known to scare off evil spirits and I doubt any amount of sage will get rid of this thing. I can only toss and turn in my bed, trying to ignore his malicious presence.

Don't you want to see your little cats again? You are not wanted or loved here. Don't you just want to be with them again?

The harsh voice that suddenly went through my head made me jump, I didn't recognize the voice in my head and the sound of it sounded threatening and raspy.

"Please..... Just....Gooooo awaaaaaay." I can only plead with it. I'm certain that if this thing doesn't kill me in whatever sick way it decides that I will go mad from sleep deprivation alone.

Don't you just want to end it all? Don't you want a friend in me? I can be your friend. I can look after you.

I curl my body up into a ball and hug my soft blankets close to my chest as I try to breathe in the smell of my cats. I haven't been able to bring myself to wash the blankets that they slept on with me because the smell of them is literally all I have left now.

I try so hard to focus on the soft blankets that still carry the scent and fur of both of my cats and I try to block out the sound of the heavy breathing next to my ear.

"Leave me alone... " I tried to whisper at whatever this thing was lying next to me in my bed and at that point I felt the bed creak as whatever it was got up and left. I felt grateful, maybe that was it and maybe the spirit didn't want to harm me and was only trying to provide comfort for me in the only way it knew.

I was shaking but felt a bit better now that whatever it was had left. I decided maybe this was the same spirit that had been following me since I was a little girl and that it had good intentions for me but didn't know it was creeping me out.

I just didn't like the feeling of being stalked by something that I could not see. Maybe I was only afraid because I couldn't communicate with it until now.

I forced myself to smile slightly as I hugged the blankets to my chest and breathed in particles of old cat fur. I knew it may have been gross but I didn't care and it was my way of grieving.

I heard it then, the purring of my cats and I opened my eyes expecting to see the cats. Maybe I had finally connected with them and could communicate with their spirits now!

I opened my eyes, expecting to see the cats but there was nothing there.

"Got you" it finally spoke aloud.

ABOUT THE AUTHOR

Natasha Godfrey

Natasha Godfrey is an Australian scare actor, support worker and horror enthusiast who stumbled into the writing world after tumbling down the freelance writing rabbit hole.

Natasha has overcome personal demons to write and publish books on Amazon including Recovering From Self Harm -By a Recovering Self Harmer and Burn that Trauma Bond and as a horror enthusiast is obsessed with horror.

Natasha has also worked with Endless Ink Publishing House and has completed online work through the platform Upwork which was the platform she used to commence her freelance journey.

Writing aside, Natasha is a crazy cat lady, coffee junkie and creative weirdo.

STORY 2

The Real Mr. Sandman

I can't take it anymore.... I don't know how to live with myself. The nightmares.... they're never ending.... It's all too much. I haven't had a restful sleep in around... I think 4 months?

I haven't counted the days really, I don't think I even remember what the time is anymore. But one thing is for sure, I will never close my eyes ever again, or else... I'd go back there.

Roughly months ago, I think, was the time it happened. It was the first day of my endless nightmare, the day I wish I could take it all back. I should've been more careful... but I could have never expected this to happen.

I was in high school; my friends and I were chatting with each other, gossiping, telling high tales. The usual teen stuff, it was just an average day really. But a week before that, Carol, the occult club leader was taken to a mental ward last week for voluntarily refusing to sleep. We don't know much about the details of her condition, but it got the students chatting and gossiping.

The official reason provided by the school authorities was that Carol was merely overstressed by her studies and daily life balance, and she'd go back to normal as soon as possible, and had attempted suicide. However, one of my friends, Jennifer told me an explanation about a particular demon that could have caused Carol's current state.

She was part of the occult club too, it wasn't an official club actually but an under the nose type club recruited in an underground sort of fashion, and Jennifer said that Carol was messing around with spirits or demons. It was definitely not a typical conversation.

She said that Carol was obsessed with finding an image of a demon named Nip; the real Mr. Sandman. I noticed what she called it, Mr. Sandman, and asked for further elaboration. Apparently, Nip was the demon that inspired the mythological Mr. Sandman as we know it, and he was far more malevolent.

Our conversation was cut short when the teachers were passing by us, we couldn't really discuss more but she invited me to the occult club meeting place, which would be the chess club's room at night. I really don't want to be around in school after hours, especially after what happened to Carol. But she kept pestering me, and I gave in to the pressure.

It was after school, and we stuck around in the chess club after the members had left. Carol had hidden her notes inside a dent in the wall, and Melissa retrieved them. I asked where were the other members, but she said that she is the only remaining one after the incident, the rest were too frightened to be in the club after what happened with Carol

Melissa told me that she was sure this was the demon responsible for Carol's condition and she wanted my help since there was no one left to help. I reluctantly agreed despite my common sense, but I didn't know what I'd do, I don't know anything about demons.

She provided me the notes and I crossed checked almost all of them. They were all written by Carol with her signature, and they're all purely text, describing Nip and who he was. Carol was obsessed with this "demon" because of a rumor she herself heard online.

According to her notes, Nip was one of the vilest creatures on the planet. Enjoying sadistic torture and controlling its victims, Nip loved violence and craved for it. One account of him was that Nip was ripping the flesh of a young child it kidnapped with its fingernails, and then proceeded to place a large knife under her eye... and it'd proceed to... I couldn't bear to read it anymore.

Melissa pestered me to read on more, and I did. Nip apparently was imprisoned by unknown forces who successfully banished it away from the material realm, our world. It now resides in another dimension and it only exists here in its imagery. It now tries to find a way into our world... through any means possible.

I was shocked, did this thing tortured Carol? But no one reported of any injuries on Carol... then Melissa nudged me to look into something, a picture of something and a paper. I shouldn't have done that.

The picture was of a black figure that was thin like a stick. The eyes were missing, the nose was missing and ears were missing. It has no facial features, no fingers and no toes, save for a very, very wide smile. That smile, sent shivers down my spine, it had no eyes and yet the one thing that stared into me was its smile.

I looked back at Melissa, and she was just staring at me. I continued reading, and I was dumbfounded for what I read. Nip has used the power of its image to render fear into anyone that knows its nature, and if combining its imagery with the horror it can bring... it will be alive to that person. And it will live inside you, until it decides to leave you.

I looked at Melissa, and she had that same big wide smile like Nip had on the photo. There was an immense chill into my spine, and I just pushed her down to the ground, and she did not resist. I ran away from her as fast as possible. What kind of prank was this?

I can't think straight, it felt like a joke. A "demon" that would live inside of me? I can't think straight. I ran back to my house, where my father was waiting for me. I told him I'd be late to study with my friends, of course it was a lie but he wasn't any the wiser. But my father noticed my expression and asked me what was wrong.

I couldn't give an answer; I felt like I couldn't give it to him. I couldn't formulate my thoughts. My dad told me that my eyes were baggy and recommended me some sleep. I didn't object, I was mentally exhausted by that sick prank. Why would Melissa do this? I just don't understand...

I went to my bedroom, and fell flat onto the bed. But I couldn't sleep, not yet, the lights were on. And I got back up to turn them off, and as soon as I did that, I heard laughter. A chittering laugh, like it was right behind me. I turned the lights on and no one was there.

I thought it was my mind playing tricks on me, but it felt like something was near. I turned the lights off again, and then immediately I see something standing in front of me in the shroud of darkness. I looked at it for a while and then it RAN straight for me. I turned the lights on once again and it disappeared.

I didn't know what to do, I decided to leave the lights on and I dismissed it as a hallucination. I once again planted my face onto the bed, and decided to sleep... and then I woke up, or at least I thought I woke up. Instead of my bedroom, I woke up in a dark area, where there's nothing the eye can see for miles around. No elevation, no features, just darkness.

It was an open area devoid of anything except the dark, as well as the hard floor that I was sitting on. I looked around, and when I turned my head to the left, something on the corner of my eye ran past me. I followed it using my head, and it kept running, I did this over and over, until I looked straight.

I saw then, a dark humanoid figure, standing tall over me with a wide big smile, and he had no other facial features. I was looking at Nip. He cackled, he didn't say a word. The way he looked in this world much realer than what I could see in the normal world, it was like he was reality and I'm staring into a malevolent reality.

I felt a sharp pain in my hip, so sharp I fell to the ground in agony. He didn't even do anything, and he did do something at once. I couldn't comprehend it On the one hand, he didn't move, on the other, I felt something that I just knew it must come from him. It was unexplainable, But I knew he caused it not by logical reasoning, but because I was consciously forced to.

And then later, I heard a voice, my own voice, asking me if I renounce anything I know and love. I don't understand, but the pain was unbearable, I just said yes. The pain lightened, and it seemed it was giving me mercy.

That was until, the once open room, closed in itself. It kept shrinking and shrinking, and Nip was nowhere to be seen. The walls, floors and ceiling kept closing in to me; until it was so cramped I could barely move my fingers, and just my fingers.

I was in so much pain, I couldn't do anything. I couldn't bang against the wall, the floor or ceiling. When I tried to scream, I left out nothing but air. When I tried to reason, it didn't answer. The one thing I was allowed to do was think. I was fully conscious at this moment, I was fully aware.

Actually, I felt even more aware than I ever was at this moment in time. Everything was real and it felt much worse than in the real world. I felt the same sharp pain in my hip again, but then I felt it in my back, my chest and my head.

The punishment was agonizing, I wanted to wake up as I thought it was a nightmare. But it felt like hours passed, days passed, and possibly a week and I was being tormented by a cackle all the while with no lightening of the pain I was inflicted.

I could barely breathe, and at that point I wanted to die or wake up. I couldn't take it anymore, and then my pain suddenly became even worse, and it felt like my body was being vaporized while I was conscious. I tried to scream to no avail, it kept getting worse and worse, until I finally did it. I let out a scream, and then I woke up.

I woke up to see the lights on, and I was back in the real world. But I kept screaming, and my father burst into my room. Although it was my father, I kept screaming, because I can finally do so. I can finally speak and scream. But what I didn't want to do was feel, I felt so much already.

All the hardship I suffered here before was nothing compared to it. I didn't want to be back there. I was a sobbing mess. My father drove me to the hospital to check on my mental health, but on the way, I dozed off for a second. And that second, I was back in that same nightmare world, and the same thing happened, for three days. And when I woke up again, only a second had passed.

I realize now, that sleep was the cause, and that for each second I sleep in the real world, it would equate to a much longer time there,

Nips world. I didn't know what to do, except never sleep again. When I arrived at the clinic, I explained what happened, but the doctors merely said I was suffering from a sleep disorder.

They didn't take me seriously, I knew what happened. I don't want to go back. I vow not to spend any time there, so I vowed to never sleep again. And I successfully did this for four months. This is how we finally got here. I did it by scarring myself each time with a kitchen knife when I felt sleepy.

My father wanted to take me to psychiatric care, but I threatened to take my life by slitting my own throat and to be honest that'd sounds appealing. But what happens if I die, if sleep means that world...dying could be worse for me... I want to stay alive... but I have to remain awake.

My eyes are red, my father had begged me to stop this, but I can't. When he left me alone, I can hear his sobbing. But I paid no mind, I focused on not sleeping. It's been this way for months now I think, and I think I'm doing it well. I'm motivated by my desire to never go to that world again. I felt successful, and I began to smile, a wide smile.

Then...I remembered Melissa and wondered what happened to her... why did she do this to me? I felt like something must've happened to her. The same thing? I can't think anymore... this thinking is tiring... I went for months without sleep, and it's not possible to sustain being awake any longer.

I don't want to do this anymore; I think I'm not going to take any chances. I placed the knife under my face, and my body gave up from exhaustion. I fell under the knife, face first still conscious. I finally felt like I escaped my fate... but before I closed my eyes, I saw nip,

standing before me one last time... or is the last? I... I don't know...
I don't know now; did I really escape? It's getting blurry...

ABOUT THE AUTHOR

Zairol Adham Bin Zainuddin

Hey there, It's me, Zairol.

I'm a guy who likes to write. Why do I like to write? Because writing is easy, look how easy it is to put words like I am doing right now. All I have to do is move my fingers on a keyboard or tablet and words come out. Simple as that.

I have studied commerce, and have taken a keen interest in the medical field, I hope one day to further myself in the field of medicine but as of right now, I'd like to gain some experience in the field of creative, content and copy-writing.

Now aside from talking about me and my dreams, what have I done previously? In terms of writing I made a complex murder story and have made a few guides here and there on certain video games. It's a lot more work than you think, but I enjoy doing it and I learnt a lot from it.

That's all there is of the current, If you want to know more about me, go ahead and message me and I'll shoot a reply. Maybe we can discuss work opportunities and we'll be able to collaborate together.

zairoladham@gmail.com

www.linkedin.com/in/zairol-adham-bin-zainuddin-6a350826b (LinkedIn)

STORY 3

The Choice Is Yours

In this life, I have learned two important things. Number one is that our choices define us, and number two is that a pretty girl in your bed can fix almost anything.

Like most people, I've made some less-than-ideal choices in my life. These choices have led me to this moment, sitting in the bathroom, contemplating everything that led me here.

I keep asking myself if this is really the way I thought I would end up. As I walk out of the bathroom, I notice that the sun is shining across the length of my bedroom. I sigh as I itch my stubble and stumble back over to the bed. I try to put all of the pieces of last night together, but my piercing headache as a result of my hangover makes that hard.

As I sit back down on the bed, I reach over to the beautiful redhead I had met the night before. I brush the hair out of her face as she lays motionless, sheets pulled up and over her chest. Her soft, pale skin looks even more beautiful this morning than it did last night when I met her at the bar. I wish I could remember her name.

Nowadays, I bring so many girls home that I tend to forget their names. Would my sister think less of me if she knew I treated women as objects? I push those thoughts down as my mind begins to humanize this woman lying in my bed. I once again get up and walk over to the kitchen.

There's no mess throughout the house this time. Only my bedroom saw the impact with some pillows on the floor and stains on the sheets. My body aches as I realize, I don't recover from a night of drinking as I used to. I'm really getting too old for this now. My bad decisions are becoming worse by the way.

My thoughts take over once again, so I hastily walk over to the kitchen sink and splash my face with ice-cold water. I knew that the water wouldn't fix my problems, but it awakens me for now. I look back over to the beautiful woman in my bed, still enjoying her rest. The sun really shows me how beautiful she is. She's almost like an angel.

I crack open a new can of beer and head towards my freezer. I open it and feel the cool air against my face as it embodies me. I smile to myself as I lean inside and greet the three beautiful heads looking back at me. They were lifeless now, but still completely beautiful just as they were when they were alive.

I don't remember their names anymore, but what else do you expect from me? I say hello to the girls with excitement, knowing my beautiful redhead will soon be with them. I'm sure they will all become quite good friends. As I close the freezer, I head back to the girl in my bed who was waiting for my return.

Why do I do this knowing I'm going to have to spend the entire day cleaning up my own mess? At least the blood stains are only on my sheets this time. The last girl was messy.

I quickly peel the covers off the lifeless woman who is still shining in the glorious morning sun. Her body has begun to sag now from all of the puncture wounds I left on her before I tucked her in for a good night's sleep. Now, I have to clean.

One Month Later

I can't believe I'm doing this again. I'm back in a bar, searching the crowd for someone memorable, and downing yet another drink that will contribute to my hangover in the morning. I think about my choices and how they led me here.

Then, I spot a stunning leggy brunette from across the bar. She would look beautiful next to my other girls in the freezer. While most men here tonight are searching for romance, I'm hunting for a trophy. The brunette makes her way across the room.

She hops up next to me at the bar and doesn't even gaze in my direction for a moment. Her big, innocent brown eyes look up at the bartender as her hair falls across her face. She is effortlessly beautiful, and she doesn't care about a single person's attention in this bar. She is here for herself. I like that, it's rare.

She turns to see me staring at her and offers me a look of disgust. Nervous, I stand up and decide to wait for her outside. I weave through the ocean of bodies on the dance floor and head out the door. It's nice and quiet out here and it's better she doesn't think I'm stalking her.

She needs to find interest in me. I light a cigarette and lean against the wall as I wait for my prey to exit the bar. As I take the last drag, I see her exit the bar typing furiously on her phone. Who is she texting? She begins walking and I look around to ensure that no one is nearby so I can follow her.

As I'm following her, I think more about choices. Her choice to walk home alone tonight will likely be the last choice she ever makes. As I get lost in my thoughts, the street becomes quieter, and the lights become more varied. She is still lost in her text conversation as I set my hand down ready to grab my knife.

I'm not far from her at this point; I can smell her perfume from here. I'm so lost in my own thoughts that I only just notice two shadows enter from an alleyway right in front of my target. I back off right away and jump into the next shallow cove in the alleyway.

As I watch, the two men back her into the side of the alley. She lets out a sharp gasp as her back hits the wall. One draws out a weapon. From this far back, I'm not sure if it is a gun or a knife, but I know that he tends to do damage with it. "Give us your purse, now", the taller man grunts.

I'm frustrated at this point, wondering what to do if I can't take this woman home tonight. I keep telling myself to walk away, but her scream catches me again. She is fighting for her life at this point. I picture her in my mind, effortlessly gliding through the bar. "Choices", I mutter to myself.

And with that, I forget any sane thought and head towards the men. As I make my way towards the shorter man, he briefly looks up before I bring my knife to his throat. With little resistance, I cut through his airway like butter. I feel the flesh resist against my blade as I feel the warmth of his blood against my chest. I drop him onto the floor as I head over to the next man who is watching me in fear.

Much to my disbelief, he musters up the strength to stand and meet me. I now recognize that it is a knife in his hand, and it is much smaller than mine. His hands are shaking as he brings his blade up towards me. He lunges suddenly, but misses me completely. I take this chance to plunge my knife into his chest.

He catches my eye as he realizes the severity of his choices on this night. I know he won't die immediately, but he will succumb to his wounds in a short while. As soon as I think this is over, I turn to the brunette, eyes wide with fear. Before I can step towards her, I feel a hand grip my ankle.

He was too weak to hold on, but the act alone infuriated me. I pick up his small knife and plunge it into his abdomen as I hear the flesh being carved. When I see him become immobile, I know that he is dying. Covered in blood, I turn towards the brunette as I hear her whimpering in the corner.

I walk over and reach my hand out to offer her a helping hand. She reluctantly raises her hand to mind and stands up. When I see her up close, she is even more beautiful than I remember her. She had dirt all over her face and her eyes were filled with tears. At this moment, all I could think of is that she wouldn't end up with my other girls tonight.

This situation made me realize something about choices. People deserve to choose their own fate. As I think this, I gesture towards the main street and tell her to leave. Without a word, she nods and sprints down the alley. I have no doubt her life will be very different from now on.

Six Years Later

The music floods through my ears as I check the time on my phone. This bar closes soon which makes it the ideal time to head out and wait for my next victim. I think about all the people here tonight and wonder what choices they made to end up here.

My thinking is cut short when I hear a woman's laughter cut

through the noise. Unlike normal laughter, she almost laughed like a melody. It was smooth and melodic, like nothing I had ever heard before. My eyes fall on her, and I wonder if she was carved by angels.

She had long, brunette hair that flowed down her shoulders and her back. She had an amusing smile crawling over her face as she caught me looking at her. I smile back and take a sip of my drink. Before I know it, she is walking up to me and she takes a seat. I haven't hunted for a long time now, but it is proving easy tonight, so I'm happy.

Seeing her so close to me increases my heart rate. Her big brown eyes search my entire face for some sort of reaction, but I'm frozen. *Have I forgotten how to do this?* "Do you always creep on women from the bar or am I an exception?" she playfully asks me.

I'm still taking in her beautiful features as the lights change colour around us. By the second, she only gets more beautiful. She snaps me out of my thoughts by loudly tapping her glass with her long nails. "Sorry", I mutter.

After some light chatter, she lifts her glass up to sip the remainder of her cocktail. "Do you want to get out of here?" she asks. Without hesitation, I nod. I haven't felt this urge in years, but I'm now wishing I'd brought my life with me. As we head for the door, I admire her body once again.

She is ridiculously beautiful, and the more I'm around her, the more I want her in my freezer.

"You haven't even asked my name yet", she smiles slyly as she brings her phone out from her handbag. "Don't you want to know my name?".

I smiled at her and before I could speak, she spoke over the top of me. "Amelia".

"Lucas", I answer.

I try to properly engage with her this time to distract myself from immediately grabbing the next object I find to take her life with. We make small talk once again as we walk to her apartment. As I follow her up the stairs, I notice that there are very few people around. This complex looks semi-abandoned which I'm grateful for as it may make my end goal easier if that is what I decide to do.

My thoughts cut through again. No, this is not you anymore. You can't do this again.

We finally arrive at her door, and she motions for me to follow her in. If only she knew who she was allowing to enter her safe place. As she walks in, she quickly turns around. Her beautiful, long hair brushes over her shoulder as she does so. She whispers, "I'm just going to rinse off, make yourself comfortable".

She then turned and walked off into the bathroom. As I hear the shower start, images of my last victim flood into my head. I wanted her to be in my freezer so badly. No, I'm not murdering her. It was her choice to come up to me. It is my choice to let her live. As I say, our choices define us.

I shake the thoughts out of my head and head over to the fridge to grab a beer. I don't find anything worth drinking until I spot a bottle of scotch in the back cupboard. "She has great taste", I think to myself. I hastily grab two glasses and pour generous servings into the cup.

I'm going to need more alcohol in me if I want to avoid killing this girl. Now all I needed for the drinks was some ice. As I reached for the freezer, I felt the cold air across my arm. My arm hairs stood on end for more reasons than one. In the freezer, three lifeless heads stare back at me.

I was hit with a wave of emotions. Shock, anger, respect, confusion and finally fear. This can't be happening. My stupid, fucked up choices led me to this moment. I didn't choose her she chose me. I didn't choose to kill her, but she chose to kill me.

My heart begins to pump, but before I can reach for my knife, the shower turns off and footsteps enter the kitchen.

ABOUT THE AUTHOR

Nikita Hillier

Nikita Hillier is a highly educated professional writer based in Western Australia.

She launched her full-time professional writing career back in 2018 after writing as a hobby and part-time for many years beforehand. She has a strong interest in the mental health, thriller, philosophy, pet, and lifestyle niches.

Nikita works for clients globally to create content that is unique, well-researched, and fuelled by passion. She is the ghostwriter behind several best-selling books and can't wait to publish her own books once they are finished. She is currently working on three different books and hopes to publish them in the coming years.

When Nikita isn't writing, she spends her time studying and gaining more knowledge. You can keep up to date with Nikita via the links below!

Website: https://www.nikitahillierwriter.com

Instagram: https://www.instagram.com/nikitahillierwriter/

Facebook: https://www.facebook.com/nikitahillierwriter

LinkedIn: https://www.linkedin.com/in/nikita-hillier-a66495226/

STORY 4

The Old Market Street Vendor

On a busy market street where thousands of civilians cross daily, people were unaware that a horrible crime was happening. Amidst the bustling noise, countless vehicles and colorful lights from small establishments around the area, individuals were disappearing one after another.

Files of missing reports were piling up and left unsolved as the authorities remained completely clueless about the matter. They could not find any link between the victims nor any probable cause for the crime.

All they knew was random people had suddenly disappeared, and the usual suspects had nothing to with it. The one responsible was neither the syndicates nor any human-trafficking criminals, but it was someone, or rather something, that was far beyond their wildest imagination.

Officers were assigned to man the streets while the investigation was still taking place in order to prevent any more disappearances. However, another person was taken again despite all of their vigilance.

One of the reports was from a frantic young woman who came running towards one of the officers in patrol. She said that she was looking for her boyfriend for hours. She couldn't contact his phone, and she had already walked back and forth several times from one end of the street to the other trying to find him.

They could not believe that a crime was committed right under their noses. They alerted the crowd about the situation. Sadly, some of them simply didn't care and went on with their leisure strolls.

They wanted to close down the street before anyone else could disappear. Unfortunately, blocking the path would significantly disrupt several businesses and small franchises that heavily relied on them.

The search and investigation went on for days, but they didn't find anything that could lead them to the missing individuals. Jacquelyn, the girl who lost her boyfriend, grew tired of waiting for the investigation to produce any results and had decided to act on her own.

However, the truth behind these mysterious disappearances was far worse than she could possibly handle.

Day by day, Jacquelyn returned to the area where she last saw her boyfriend. She was too worried about him that she could hardly get any sleep. From morning till night, she was asking every person that she came across. She would show them the last photo that she took with him on the day before he disappeared.

She walked along the row of vendors selling souvenirs while also asking them the same questions. Some of them were old natives that barely spoke English, and one of which was an old amputee on a wheelchair selling handcrafted trinkets and tribal displays.

His frail body was wrapped with a very large woven shawl, and he didn't have both of his legs and right arm. The old man gently smiled at her while struggling to lift his remaining left arm. His bony hand was rather large, and his fingers were extraordinarily long. He gestured towards his cart that was filled of handmade ornaments.

Out of sympathy and curiosity, Jacquelyn casually browsed through his products. They were mostly made of genuine leather stitched together, and some were of real animal bones and braided dyed fur.

Along with rattle drums, miniature masks and bone flutes, Jacquelyn's attention was drawn towards the intricately ornate leather pouches and hand stitched purses. She brushed her fingers across the braiding and noticed the leather's unique texture.

Despite all of the varnish coating, she could tell that the material was strangely softer than usual. She thoroughly inspected one of the purses, and her eyes widened as she shivered in shock when she saw a detail that was oddly familiar.

Right at the edge of the hand-sewn seams, there was a faint print on the leather that was similar to her boyfriend's tattoo. She looked closer to the print, and she found the small mole that was right below it.

She realized that the rest of his products were not of animals' skins and bones. Her knees buckled, and she knocked one of the rattles off the cart. When it shattered on the floor, she discovered that the contents of the rattle were smashed pieces of human teeth.

She almost vomited when she realized that she was holding a purse that was made out of her boyfriend's own skin. She hesitantly panned her eyes towards the old vendor, and he was looking back at her with a sickening grin on his face.

Before she could call for help, her body suddenly froze and her consciousness went hazy. In a blink of an eye, Jacquelyn disappeared from the street without anyone noticing.

A couple of individuals had also gone missing since Jacquelyn's disappearance. Just like hers, there were also more victims in the past that wasn't reported to the authorities.

Officer Geoffrey was assigned to handle the case, and he was willing to take some drastic measures in order to stop it from happening. He dispatched three of his men to disguise as civilians in hopes of luring in the criminal.

In a busy night when people were coming from different places, the officers blended in and walked around like commoners within the crowd while relaying what they were seeing to Geoffrey through their earpieces.

Nothing seemed odd at the beginning, and a young officer in disguise named Dustin just browsed through the stalls until he reached the souvenir stands. Based on some of the reports, this was the area where they last saw some of the victims.

Drowned by the noise of the people and the vendors calling out to their customers, Dustin concentrated his inspection around the area while having some difficulties relaying information clearly. He casually walked along like a common passerby browsing on the souvenir items until he reached the cart of the old vendor on the wheelchair.

Out of curiosity, he asked him how he could move his cart on his own despite of his challenged condition, but the old man just smiled at him without saying anything. All of a sudden, Dustin stopped reporting to Geoffrey.

The other officers immediately rushed towards his last reported location, but all they found was his earpiece on the ground. They heard him describing an old vendor before he stopped talking, but the mentioned man and his cart were gone.

For an old amputee on a wheelchair, it was quite strange how fast he was able to get away from the scene. However, he was not aware that all of the officers in disguise were equipped with tracking devices. Officer Geoffrey foresaw this exact situation, and they hurriedly traced Dustin's pinpointed location.

They were led to an alley that wasn't too far from the area. Nobody would usually go to this spot since it was closed down years ago and in between two abandoned buildings. Inside the alley, they found the old vendor's cart in front of a makeshift tent made of torn cardboard and tarp.

The officers unholstered their firearms and called him out, but he did not respond. Geoffrey inspected the vendor's abandoned cart, and he discovered that the side of the cart was an empty compartment with a spring door where someone could easily slide in.

He was carrying the victims inside his cart which made it look like they were suddenly disappearing from the street, but it would still take some serious skill in order to do it without being noticed.

Geoffrey still couldn't fathom how an old guy on a wheelchair was able to do all this on his own. He was also wondering how he was taking his victims since there was no trace of blood or any sign of struggle inside the cart.

The officers went inside the tent and saw the old vendor's wheelchair. There were holes on the seat as if it was pierced by a spear several times over. They also discovered a cellar door that would lead them under the abandoned building.

They could no longer detect Dustin's tracking device, but it was clear where they had to go next. Geoffrey had dealt with strange and inhumanely cruel cases throughout his years, but none of his previous experiences could have possibly prepared him for the kind of horror that he was about to face.

When they opened the cellar door, they were greeted by a foul stench of rotting flesh and potent chemicals coming from below. Along with two armed officers, Geoffrey immediately climbed down to search for the criminal. The chronic smell was so potent that they had to cover their noses as they moved ahead.

The floor was sticky because of the layers of dried blood that accumulated for a long time. When they reached the first room of the cellar, one of the officers vomited because of what they saw. It was a gallery of disembodied human corpses hanged on the walls and hooked on the tables like an unkempt butcher's kitchen.

Their skins were peeled off from their bodies and dried under a light. Their hairs were collected on a loom and braided manually like woven belts and bracelets. Their eyes and teeth were removed and collected on jars like pickles and beads.

Unfortunately, they weren't able to save Officer Dustin. His lifeless body was hooked like a slab of meat with his blood flushing down the drain. This indescribable hellhole was significantly worse than what Geoffrey could have possibly imagined. He thought that only a heartless fiend could commit such an inhumane crime, and this statement was accurate in several ways.

The officers cautiously proceeded to the next section, and there they saw the merciless criminal at work. He was sitting right in his workshop, and Jacquelyn's skin was hanging on a coat rack right beside him.

The room was filled with preserved limbs, skins, and other parts that were modified in a way to compose grotesque forms of his own creation.

The peculiarity of this merciless culprit was in sordid display like a sickening artistry which he was clearly proud of, and his materials were exclusively of human parts.

Aside from the inexplicably horrid things around them, they noticed a strange slender limb sticking out from the old man's amputated right arm. It functioned like a replacement as he was effectively threading a needle with it.

Disgusted, frightened yet enraged at the same time, Geoffrey and the two other officers pointed their guns to arrest him. Yet despite all of their authoritative yelling, he remained seated and was completely unfazed.

Given the situation, Geoffrey bypassed the proper method of arrest and decided to fire his gun at the table as warning shot. This bold action had indeed triggered a reaction from the criminal, but the unexpected turn that happened next was an image of nightmare taking form right before their eyes.

Four long tubular limbs that were akin to a spider's legs suddenly sprout out from the old man's bottom, and he turned to them while rising from his seat like a disturbed quadrupedal beast. His amputated legs did not matter for he had more than enough to stand taller than an average man.

His right arm that replaced his human arm were significantly longer and had seven long fingers with deadly sharp nails. Completely terrified and in disbelief, the officers immediately open fired while backing away.

Unfortunately, this appalling entity was far quicker than they thought. Before they could turn away, he swiftly crawled towards one of the officers and stared at him face to face. The officer was suddenly frozen in place and couldn't move a single finger.

This creature could petrify his target just by looking at them directly, and that was how he was able to snatch his victims from the street without any resistance at all. Aside from this unnatural ability, his abnormal arm was unbelievably quick.

Geoffrey and the other officer kept on firing and did not move their sight from this hellish fiend, but they didn't even notice what he did. The next thing they saw was a gush of blood from their fellow officer's neck, and his head rolled over the floor. His head was cut clean in just a fraction of a second, and none of them was able to do anything about it.

This humanoid arachnid lunged towards Geoffrey. He was about to petrify him, but he swiftly moved away when the other officer aimed for a head shot. Geoffrey realized that a shot on the head would bring him down, but it was easier said than done. He was able to jump out of the way when the fiend tried to decapitate his head as well.

He reacted as fast as he possibly could, and he missed his neck by just a hair. Geoffrey said to the remaining officer to aim for the monster's head as he ran towards him. He figured that he could only petrify one target at a time, and he had to pause for a second in order stare into his eyes.

They leaned on a wall and aimed for his head side by side, the spiderlike beast had no other choice but to attack them head on. They emptied their magazines, but he was moving too fast and they weren't able to hit the mark.

As Geoffrey reloaded his gun, the beast took this opportunity and hastily attacked. He spiked Geoffrey's leg with his front limb as he stared at the other officer closely. He was able to petrify him, but this was the opening that Geoffrey was waiting for. He endured the pain and reloaded his gun, and he shot the fiend's head point blank while he was focused on the other officer right beside him.

The case of the missing people was finally closed. Two officers lost their lives in the process, and no single victim was saved. The operation might be seen as a failure to some people, but they were able to spare the lives of any future victims.

The case was not disclosed to the public in order to prevent panic and unwanted attention. Officer Geoffrey and the others who saw the horrifying things inside that cellar will never forget this particular case, and the body of the criminal was taken to a special facility in order to study it.

ABOUT THE AUTHOR

Saint Quinn

A writer and an illustrator, Saint Quinn has ghost-written short stories and short novels for starting authors and narrators in various platforms.

With a writing experience of more than five years, he wrote over a hundred stories under horror and science fiction genres.

Saint Quinn's stories often feature bizarre and unconventional creatures instead of popular icons of the genre, and the disparity between normal humans to these original characters are vividly portrayed throughout his stories.

With more attention to depicting helplessness and despair rather than heroic acts of remarkable human protagonists, the horrors of Saint Quinn does not focus in explaining relatable situations but the unprecedented events of terror to the unknowing. As an illustrator, the majority of his artworks are macabre.

Website:

https://www.teepublic.com/user/saintquinn

STORY 5

Demon Bed

"Goddamn bed!"

"Pivot Jim, otherwise we'll be here all day long."

"I told you, Maddy, we ought to have taken it apart, brought it inside, and *then* put it back together. Look at us, we've barely made it into the house and already we're half dead… There's no way we'll make it up the stairs, it's literally impossible."

"It's an antique Jim, there's no manual to help us assemble it back together once we take it apart, and if memory serves me right, It was you who turned down that nice gentleman's offer to have it deposited right inside the bedroom and at no extra cost whatsoever…"

"*Nice*? Do you hear yourself? Maddy, that guy was a fucking creep. Who the hell offers post-buy services for second-hand sales? A friggin' weirdo, that's who"

"Don't be daft. He was a nice old man and as a matter of fact, I've half a mind to give him a call…"

Jim almost collapsed from the weight of the huge six-by-six mahogany bed as Maddy, his lovely girlfriend, abruptly let go of the end she was barely holding up and walked out of the room, her ginger hair flowing angrily behind her.

"Alright then, murder me with the ten-ton bed and move in with the 'nice' old gentleman from the antique shop, *that'll* solve our problems…" Jim said, half to himself as he shifted his stance, slowly placing the chunky bed on the floor and staring at it,

"Man! The hell did you have for lunch?..." He added humorously.

****

"Come on babe, I said I'm sorry…"

"Yeah, and I said, we're good."

"Alright, how about we go get ice cream and maybe some chocolate while the creepy nice guy and his crew go about sorting out our bed problem, how does that sound?"

"Sounds like you owe me a lot more than chocolate and ice cream," Maddy said, throwing Jim a foxy look which he picked up instantly.

"Dzaam Maddy! But I thought you said the couch was uncomfortable…" He replied playfully.

"Who said anything about a couch? Plus I happen to recall a perfectly functional renaissance-era big-ass mahogany bed sitting in the middle of our dining room…"

Maddy moved toward Jim and grabbed his shirt pulling him down toward her face.

"Hell yeah, come here…" Jim wrapped his arms around Maddy's waist and pulled her toward himself, kissing her slightly parted lips, and felt her melt into his arms. He loved how supple her body felt against his, and enjoyed the soft imperceptible moans that issued from deep inside her.

Jim's mind wandered and half centered on the sensual flames eating away at him, man did he love Maddy, he thought to himself. Then suddenly, Maddy's soft and warm body stiffened and her eyes grew wide and alert.

"Did you hear that?" She asked in a half-whisper.

"Hear what honey... come here, you was saying something about a renaissance-era bed..."

"I think it came from the dining room" Maddy went on, oblivious to Jim's efforts at rekindling a rapidly diminishing flame. Jim moaned in protest as Maddy pushed him away and started toward the dining room;

"Did you leave the sliding doors to the dining room open?" She asked. Her face looked concerned and a certain ominous urgency hung to her voice as she addressed her partner.

"It's probably just Dog, I think he's learning how to unlock doors..." He was slumped over the kitchen table, trying to shift his mind's attention from the pulsing mass of penis in his pants.

Despite the seemingly detached name he had christened the massive six-year-old Saint Bernard, Jim loved the dog (he treated Dog like a whole other human being; It even had its couch in the living room). It was one of the things that Maddy loved about her boyfriend. The other thing was his interesting sense of humor – at the moment, she hated his guts so much she wanted to cry.

"I'm serious Jim, I heard something thud in there."

Dog *did* know how to work around doors and Jim loved gloating about it. But this time, he decided not to pursue it. He knew Maddy, and he knew how volatile the situation was. He chose instead to follow Maddy into the dining room to check out the thud.

"I told you, honey, there's nothing in here…" Jim said, his eyes darting around the room. Maddy peeked suspiciously from behind him, her feet on tip-toe as if afraid to offset the artificial peculiarity she felt seeping from every inch of the room.

"What's that over there?" She said, pointing at a muddy spot near the closed sliding doors. Jim moved toward the spot and crouched over it.

"It's Dog's paw print, I told you he could unlock doors…"

"He knows how to push the bolts back in?" Maddy interrupted, her eyes gesturing toward the door lock. Jim stood up and looked around the room. His face looked puzzled as he weighed the odds, half-wondering just how proficient Dog had become at working the locks.

His gaze moved toward another inconspicuous set of muddy prints that were previously removed from his line of sight. Maddy followed Jim's gaze toward the massive four-poster and then, her curiosity getting the better of her, slowly crept up toward it.

"There's mud and dog hairs on the bed Jim." She said, her tone soft and caring but wavering. Jim rose slowly and walked to the edge of the bed. He sat on the bed and fingered the familiar tufts of hair.

"Well, I guess Dog beat us to the consecrating thing," Jim said jokingly. The forced smile on his face tried (but failed miserably) to hide the concern that gathered like a menacing storm behind his eyes, and tugged at the worry lines skirting the edges of his eyes.

Maddy, seeing the uncertainty plaguing her boyfriend, sat on the bed next to him and wrapped her hands around his wide torso. As she did she felt, more than heard, his stomach growl. A deep rumbling sound that seemed to shake the impressive bed and reverberate throughout the entire room.

"Damn babe, you Okay?" Maddy asked, fairly certain Jim had a stomach bug or something.

"That wasn't me man."

Jim looked confused as he answered... like it wasn't *his* stomach growling. Maddy felt confused as well. A second ago, she was sure Jim was just fooling around. But as she looked into his nervous, puzzled eyes, she felt a deep unbridled dread lurking around the fringes of the room. Then the doorbell rang, jerking both of them from their frightened stupor.

****

"Maddy Kaufmann?"

"That's me," Maddy replied. She peered into the doorway from behind Jim's bulking form. He held the door open but stood imposingly in the foyer, visibly obstructing whoever had rung the doorbell.

"The name's Jacques, most people just call me Jack..."

Maddy pushed Jim out of the way to welcome the old man who'd sold them the antique four-poster into the house.

"Hello, I'm Maddy. I believe we met at the store?"

"Let's see... Oh, I remember *you*! You're the nice ol' gal with the grumpy boyfriend. No offense." Replied Jack, nodding at Jim in affirmation.

"You called about the antique?" He continued, ignoring Jim's grouchy sneer.

"Yes, come on in… Where's your crew? You're not planning on moving it alone, are you? 'Cause I promise you it's a heavy eater." Maddy said lightheartedly as she beckoned him inside and led the way to the dining room.

"Oh, you don't know how much," Jack muttered under his breath.

"What's that?" Maddy asked, not quite catching Jack's words.

"…Don't you worry about it. I've moved it many times over; well not this specific bed – obviously. But many like it"

The whole time, Jim hung discreetly in the background, staring daggers at Jack. He didn't like the old antique store owner, not one bit. Aside from the unsightly scatter of matted gray hair on his head and the freakishly big mole on his wrinkled neck, Jim hated how he made him feel. He didn't have the words to explain it; but he felt a sort of guarded dread whenever he was around him… like how one feels when walking through a cemetery…

"Oh, I almost forgot," Jack said, interrupting Maddy's minute explanation of the importance of pivoting, and Jim's critical thinking as well.

"Your next-door neighbor, Mrs. Crawford was it? Yeah, she wanted to talk to Jim… Said something about a Saint Bernard…"

Jim's eyes brightened at the thought of finding Dog at the Crawford's. He'd crossed into their yard many times before.

"Imma go check on Dog if that's ok, leave you guys to it ..." Jim said, addressing Maddy who nodded perceptively. I hope he hasn't fucked up Mrs. Crawford's flowerbed, he thought excitedly as he hurried out of the house, barely locking the door behind him.

His excited flurry was suddenly cut short when he saw Dog lying on his side at the edge of the yard close to the Crawford driveway. I ought to have you tagged Dog... I thought you learned your lesson the last time you ate out of Mrs. Crawford's garbage... The thoughts crossed Jim's mind conversationally as he had the familiar telepathic tête-a-tête with an oblivious Dog.

But as he walked toward his animal friend, Jim couldn't help but feel a nervous apprehension crawl its way across his skin. His pulse rate went up as his eyes, alert, seemingly picked up no movements about Dog's limp side. He felt a deep sense of dread as he slowly approached Dog's lifeless form. And then he saw it. A wide dulling crimson, spreading out from beneath Dog and covering a small patch of grass, inching its way toward The Crawford's paved driveway.

Jim stood in shock for a long minute. His eyes stared down at the beautiful black fur of his dead dog, at the dark-brown irises now turned a ghostly white, at the dark blood crusting on mowed blades of grass and loose bits of gravel.

On the surface, it seemed like his mind didn't want to comprehend the implications of the appalling scene exhibited before him, but the tears skirting the edges of his eyelids, hanging on for dear life, told another story.

Jim didn't feel anything. He had no sense of grief, felt no anger, no remorse. He had no past, no present... Only this cruel, ugly moment right here. He took off his loose-fitting cardigan and then crouching, covered the massive head and torso of his murdered dog.

In his mind, he thought, "Maddy can't see him like this." And then he remembered. Maddy! He rushed back toward the house, leaving Dog and the crime scene unattended, thinking how the hell did I leave her alone with that freak?!

Jim reached the door and slowly let himself in. He reined in his racing heart so as not to alarm Maddy lest everything was okay. And silently walked through the hallway toward the dining room.

Jim turned the corner into the dining room and immediately locked eyes with Maddy. Her eyes were screaming in terror, and her mouth was closed shut by a crudely affixed piece of duct tape. She sat on the bed at an eerie, wraithlike angle holding her hands together behind her (probably bound by something come to think of it). Her feet were seemingly concealed by the silky fabric encasing the four-poster. Jim didn't waste a second as he rushed towards Maddy, determined to sort her out of her predicament. He grabbed her face in his hands and gingerly ripped the duct tape off her frightened face.

"THE BED'S A FUCKING DEMON, JIM!" Maddy's voice tore hysterically into the room, shattering the uncanny silence floating about. Jim's eyes flitted around in confusion as he tried to make sense of just what was going on.

"Calm down Maddy? What do you mean demon? Who did this to you?"

Jim didn't get his answer. Instead, he felt a blunt stabbing pain at the back of his head and the room spun around, and suddenly he was crashing into the ground hitting his head on the stocky hardwood foot of the bed as he went – knocked out cold.

Maddy's eyes gaped in shock at the collapsed body of her boyfriend. Perceiving a freakish amount of blood pooling around his head, her expression fell and the tears that came obstinately shook her so. She felt more defeated than confused.

Jack, the odd store owner, had jumped her the moment Jim got out of the house. For some unusual reason, he seemed certain that her boyfriend wasn't coming back for a while. He tied her up and gagged her with duct tape then tossed her onto the four-poster.

And then horror of horrors, Maddy started sinking into the bed like she was stuck in quicksand. She had no clue what the hell was going on and the gleeful sneer on that fucking antique store guy only served to enrage her further.

Suddenly, Jim appears in the doorway and their eyes lock, and Maddy tries as best she could to scream and wriggle and blink and scream again, frantically trying to warn Jim of what he was walking into. But Jim rushed toward her either way. I mean what *did* she expect him to do? How was he supposed to know? She thought bitterly to herself. Suddenly there he was, ripping off the duct tape, unaware of the danger.

Maddy screamed something about a demon bed (as she reminisced, she hated herself for not instead warning him of Jack) and Jim stared at her, not quite getting what she meant. And now there he was; bleeding out at the foot of a bed they didn't even need, at the hands of a guy who he didn't even like.

Maddy's thoughts were cut short when Jack walked into the room holding in his hands Jim's limp Saint Bernard. Maddy had already sunk out of sight. She couldn't feel her limbs, and her head and neck were the only parts of her still visible.

She felt she could give no more as she saw Dog's matted bloody fur. But a stiff shriek rose from the confused grief poking at her guts. And as her head disappeared into the silky sheets, Maddy belted out a last distraught wail that was muffled instantly.

****

Jack heaved Jim's dead body into the bed next to the half-sunk Saint Bernard, and then he took a stumpy hunting knife from his coat pocket and tossed it onto the bed. The girlfriend had already disappeared into the infinite bounds of the four-poster. The heavy dog and its owner would go even faster. It would take about a month for the house to go on the market, he thought to himself.

"I'll come get you then." He said to the bed, before walking into the hallway and out of the house, locking the door behind him.

ABOUT THE AUTHOR

Edwin Onserio

Onserio is a student and ghostwriter from Nairobi, Kenya. He freelances on Upwork and especially enjoys writing Horror fiction, Thrillers, Spicy romances and everything in between.

He's big on Rock music and is a huge fan of Haruki Murakami. Aside from reading books he enjoys collecting old stuff – He was born in 2001 so his idea of 'old stuff' spans anything pre-1999.

He's the proud owner of a Sony Walkman WM-34, and a Saw 2004 VHS Tape.

Contact him on Upwork via the link below:

Upwork freelancer:

https://www.upwork.com/freelancers/~01c1aacf309dceac9e

STORY 6
Iceberg Deep

A few people disappeared every night. Through the foggy ice enveloping the hull of the ship, they disappeared. Last night, I've seen the reason for our expedition to the arctic, Mr. Whitman, a very rich and eccentric author, making his way towards the iceberg which was around a few hundred meters away.

Everyone was talking about that iceberg under their breaths when the deck wasn't too crowded. It raised my curiosity as well. I caught myself standing on the cold corridors of the ship and looking at the iceberg through the circular windows.

The iceberg had the shape of a miniature mountain, miniature in the sense that it was still colossal, many times larger than the ship, but still was smaller compared to an actual mountain. It stood alone with the flat ice surrounding every direction all the way to the horizon. Its lone nature caught the eye, with no other icebergs, hills, or anything similar in sight.

I knew people didn't want to believe the disappearances were happening because of it. When the crew talked, they talked about the impossibility of survival if they left the ship. The ones who gave up a few days ago knew deep down that the chance of survival on the ship was around the same, but most kept quiet.

The ship broke down 8 days ago. As we tried our best to keep the ice away and fix the problems, the ice got to us anyway. We were stuck, with no way to move. Breaking the ice to move forward was unlikely, as we had learned in our attempts.

We were now waiting for rescue, a rescue that we didn't call for, couldn't call for, as no signal reached out to anything that could hear us.

I saw Whitman leave the ship, go down to the ice, and walk towards the iceberg. He had his satchel full of notebooks, as he always did. I looked at him walking on the ice, with the determination of a man in search of new information. The moonlight danced inside the ice, illuminating him from both directions, making him seem almost like he was in a stage, in a play.

I followed behind him the day after. During the regular stock checks, I came to realize that the food would run out rather quickly, and even though the crew and the passengers only got smaller in numbers as the days went on, tensions were rising, and after one of the mechanics got stabbed, I knew our time was coming to an end.

I wanted to look only, get close, and see how it looked like up-close, maybe even take a small chunk of it. I knew it would melt, but the desire to take a piece from this huge mass was powerful; and so, I went.

Now, in the glory of the giant before me, I saw the darkness that went on endlessly, at the base of the mountain. It was a huge opening that went down in a downwards slope only barely steep enough to safely walk on.

I looked behind me, at the ship. It was still there; it would only take 10 or so minutes to go back. There should have been around 40 people left in the ship by now, almost half the population from the time we left shore.

Half of the population was ahead of me, close to 40 people, down in that darkness. What did they find, an icy death? It wouldn't hurt to go forward carefully, and to see what happened. The cold air was almost blowing me towards the cavern entrance, pushing me towards it as I knew every step taken back to the ship would be as consuming as taking a hundred steps forward. So, rather than waiting for my ultimate doom in the metal coffin stuck in the arctic, I decided to delve into the unknowns of the earth, with the hope that I would come back out.

The cave was cold, but not as much as the outside was. Sheltered from the harsh winds as sharp as a steel knife, I pressed forward, taking care of every single one of my steps with the care that I would take if I was walking on tightrope.

The floor was slippery, and though my gear was more than equipped enough to handle my surroundings, great care was still needed. The floor became less sloped after a while, with it becoming suddenly more than I expected. I took one step too much and too hastily, taken in complete darkness aside from the flashlight barely illuminating my way, I slipped and started to tumble downwards.

My mind raced but no thought was present. I tried to grab onto anything to slow my fall, but nothing was there, I tumbled towards the bottom as every half flip made my body scream in pain.

As I tried to create a wide area using my hands to slow my fall with friction, with anything that my body was instinctually doing in that moment, nothing worked. Then, the slope came to a fast and unexpected end as my whole body gave its weight to my left arm, falling on top of it.

The cracking sound echoed through the darkness as I felt the sharp pain go through my body like a sizzling electric shock. With disorientation, pain, and confusion, I tried to catch my breath. I was on my knees, my body hunched forward as my right arm held me up.

I couldn't move the other arm. A sharp pain reverberated through my chest. As I tried to get ahold of my breathing, I knew that the moment adrenaline started to go away, the pain in my arm and ribcage would be the end of me.

I must've been there, in that pose, for a while. As my breathing slowly got slower, I could feel million sharp needles going through my body, with the biggest one going through my arm. I slowly pushed myself towards the slope that spat me here and laid my back on it. The slope was almost at a 45-degree angle. I would barely be able to walk down here even if the slope hadn't caught me off guard.

I slowly raised my head and looked at the flashlight with its cord still attached to my right, working arm. I clicked the button and even though it was prone to blinking, to my amazement, the light still worked.

I didn't know the size of the cave I was in, the floor was flat, and it went on towards all directions at least as far as the light of the flashlight let me see. I couldn't see any walls to either side or front of me. The section of the cave I was in was considerably large.

I looked around with the flashlight, to my right, to my left, up. I could see the flat ceiling, the ice reflecting the light. It was at least 5 meters high. The vast open space ahead of me unnerved me, but as the pain got worse and worse every passing second, I didn't know what to do.

I was looking at every direction, the movements of my arm getting ever-so-slightly more hectic as time went on. I knew I couldn't panic, but my body shaking from the pain wasn't helping. It was everywhere, the aching. It was on my arm, my chest, my legs, ankles, neck, head, from my fingertips to my core. I felt like I was fighting off unconsciousness.

The slope my aching back was resting on was too steep for me to climb, especially with a broken arm, but that didn't stop me from trying. I was able to get up after a long fight with my body, and after taking a single step forward and falling back down, with the pain from the fall almost making me faint, I went for another try. The second try was desperate, as it felt like I only did it to tell myself that I tried, that I tried to climb back up, but I couldn't.

My body wanted to sit down to the same position I was in before, and I listened to it, with short breaths that I would take between the streaks of pain reverberating under my skin.

Sitting back down, and my head slightly tilted left, I looked at the weak beam of light my flashlight carried around the room. I could only see a semi-cylindrical shaped opening of the darkness at a time, and everywhere I looked I saw nothing.

Until I did.

Through the veil over my eye, and barely able to keep focus, I could've sworn that I saw a figure barely escaping my light. A naked, white, and short figure. With pure panic, I tried to follow the direction where I saw it only for a split second, only to find nothing.

The second time, I saw it more clearly. It was a naked person, with skin unnaturally white and spotless. I saw it for a moment, and it escaped into the darkness. At this point, I'd lost it. I was pointing the flashlight everywhere, almost shaking it rather than holding it with intent.

With the light going across the room in a random pattern as my hand spazzed the flashlight around, I saw a lot more of them. Around a meter long, they were slowly making their way towards me, hunched back, almost as if evading detection. The darkness was now full of them.

I started screaming at them, telling them to leave me alone, pleading, saying everything my panicked mind could come up with. Even though my screaming did manage to get them back for the first time, it only helped once. I screamed and raved like I went insane, nonetheless.

I pleaded as they came even closer with their head perked up forward and knees bent, with unnaturally long arms. I asked for my mother, called out to her.

I saw one with a satchel, now only few steps away from me, and I shone the light right into its face. It had the face of a human but with slight changes. It had no nose, and unnaturally small eyes. Its mouth was long but thin, with icy white lips slightly agape. It was whispering something to me.

With eyes wide open and now in a state of frenzy and shock, I tried to keep my body as far away from it as possible, now laying down on the slope completely. It came closer, now its whisper louder, it shook its arm in front of me.

The satchel.

I screamed at it in fear and tears started flowing down from my face. The thing was taken aback for but a moment. The next moment, it held tighter to the satchel and hit my chest with it. My scream became a whisper as all air left my lungs from the impact. I tried to hold my functioning hand forward to stop the thing, but the second blow came right after the first.

As I heard the cracks coming from inside of me, no sound came out of my mouth. Few more blows came after, and light escaped my gaze, and life with it, but only for a short while, as death wouldn't come as gracefully as that.

I woke up hanging upside down. Trying to see what was around, I saw bright torches illuminate a small lake, an underground lake that I was tied above of. There was an unnatural warmness in my hair, and as I slowly touched it with my functioning hand and fingers, I felt that it was wet as well. With my hand now painted red, I looked around more. The cave around was completely empty, and something was coming towards me from the inside of the lake.

I felt everything shake and saw the dark lake below me get darker and darker as a mass of complete void rose from the unknown depths of the small lake. As the surface of the still water broke, I saw the face attached to that void.

I tried to scream, scream as loud as I could. My throat was gone, as well as most of my lungs. Only a whimper came out of my mouth before the colossal being made its way towards my body and swallowed me wh-----

ABOUT THE AUTHOR

Umut Ceylan

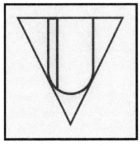

I always look forward to reading, watching, or doing anything with any type of media involving horror and the unknown. From the very tempting and almost glamorous portrayals of the underworld from the start of cinema, from how much we didn't know in the past, and how much we will know in the future, everything can be span into something terrifying to anyone. Being scared, enticed by such visions from the comfort of your couch can be almost cozy, comforting even.

I strive to write about the mysterious of many. My role models in horror include but are not limited to H.P. Lovecraft, Junji Ito, Zdzisław Beksiński, and countless other talents all over the world doing something new and terrifying but enticing and beautiful in their own twisted way at the same time.

I've been writing horror since 2010, starting with Turkish at first, I transitioned into writing in English to reach a wider audience. My goal is to entertain, and invite new worlds into our psyche, thought experiments that scratch that itch at the back of our minds.

See you there.

Other short stories:
https://medium.com/@umutceylan

You can reach me at:
umuthceylan@gmail.com

STORY 7

Stone Cold Kiss

It is embarrassing to say but it appears I have fallen for someone that I should not even dare to touch. It is an irregular love, and should anyone know of it, my dignity and reputation would be greatly affected.

However, the more I set my eyes upon her, the stronger my yearning becomes. I never thought someone like me would feel this great love - a passion, I daresay. But it happened.

I had always been a loner. I never initiated the few relationships I have, and I do not bother to maintain them. My interest lies in the one thing that I excel in - art.

My parents had always worried for me. I did not do well in school and was always in poor health. My sense in music was almost nonexistent and I had two left feet. I read books in my spare time, but even that was hardly an interest for me. It was simply a way to pass the time.

Because of the way I am, my parents constantly looked for something that could ignite a fire in me. They wanted me to find something that could give me joy, something that I could do with pride. Throughout my childhood I went through different experiences - camping, fishing, archery, dance, and piano lessons... yet none of them ever worked with me.

That was until my uncle gifted me a watercolor set on my ninth birthday. I picked up the brush and dipped it into the paint, swirling the colors on the paper. I watched, fascinated, as red combined with blues, blues melted softly with yellows... I slowly painted a beautiful picture that made my father smile and my mother gasp with excitement.

Ever since then, I immersed myself with art. I was good at it, and even more so, I enjoyed it. I even managed to expand my interests, reading books on art, philosophy and fiction to continuously give me inspiration. Finally, I found something that tickled my heart and made every day exciting.

That was how I found myself in that university. It was an old, traditional establishment that was open for young and poor alike. Different cultures and people from all walks of life gathered there to create a bustling environment of youth waiting to set out in the real world.

There, I admitted myself into the arts program. By then, I had learned how to sketch, paint, and even sculpt. My work had won me awards that gave my parents much joy. I was treated very well by my department because of my accomplishments, and that was how I was able to get into the building.

It was an old, decrepit structure. Honestly, it was pretty much abandoned. The old art building was replaced by a sturdier, modern one that housed a larger capacity of students. However, I enjoyed the quietness of the place - it was placed in a remote area of the university, surrounded by trees and shrubs that gave it a subdued atmosphere that I enjoyed.

When I worked, I preferred to be alone. It was quiet, and I could let my mind wander freely as my hands moved. No one was watching, speaking, breathing.

It was in that building that I would frequently see her. She was beautiful. Her large eyes had long lashes. She had a pronounced forehead and a small, cute nose that made her look like a delicate animal. She was petite, and her expression held a quiet mystery that I wanted to study, to understand.

She stood in the same spot by the window, the golden rays of the afternoon sun settling on her round cheeks. She is always there, unmoving.

Her empty gaze sees nothing. Her lips breathe no air. She is, alas, of stone.

I would sit in front of her, simply admiring her beauty. I would often sketch her from different angles. Sometimes I would even paint her countenance in different settings. In one, she was smiling as she sat on the riverbed. In another, she was walking in the garden, looking at a butterfly. In my work, she was very much alive, living out the best version of herself.

I know that my feelings towards her are not normal. In fact, I have deliberately avoided the attention of a girl in my class. She was tall with a buxom figure and a nice smile, but I was more drawn to the girl in the art building.

"You know, you don't have to paint everyday. Why don't we go to a coffee house sometime and exchange ideas? It could be fun," she offered one day.

"I'm afraid I don't have the time," I politely and firmly declined.

"Maybe I'll come pick you up next time," she called out as I walked away. I gave her a small wave and went on my way. She was warm and friendly, but I would rather caress that figure in the art building. I wanted to feel her cold, soothing skin against mine.

It may be arrogance, but I can't help but think that my profound love for her is what made it happen.

I was immersed in painting. This time, I was creating a submission for the upcoming competition. I was brushing deep, indigo hues on the canvass when I heard it.

A short, breathy sigh.

I looked behind me. There was no one else in the room. My heart beat faster. Was it my imagination or is someone in the room with me?

But I couldn't see anyone. I stood up and opened the door towards the hallway. I looked around, but no one was in the corridor. It was dead silent.

I went back inside and shut the door. Before returning to my work, something made me want to go up to her. I looked at her face. It was the same face. Unmoving. I shook my head and continued to paint.

Back then I simply dismissed it as my imagination. I was alone, and when you're alone in a silent room, your thoughts make things that aren't there. It paints a different reality, tricking you. Confusing you.

But over time, I felt a nagging feeling that I wasn't alone. It was as if someone was watching me. I felt a heavy feeling in the back of my head, similar to when people were watching me paint. No one spoke, but you can feel that invisible weight of expectation that made you conscious of your actions.

During those times I would look at her for strength. Somehow, it appeared as if her expression had changed. Silly, I know.

"Do you know if anyone else is using the old art building?" I asked my classmate one day.

"I don't think so," she replied.

"Are you certain? You haven't gone there, have you?"

"No. You're the only one who steps foot there. That place gives me the creeps," she said.

"Strange. Sometimes I feel like... I'm not alone."

"Don't talk like that. I'm afraid of ghosts." She gave me a gentle slap that didn't hurt one bit. I don't really get the point but somehow it made her giddier. It was a little cute.

"I'm not trying to scare you. It's just that, there's that feeling. I don't know why I'm even telling you this."

"You know, maybe it's the effect of being alone there everyday. No one to talk to," she said. Her hand remained on my arm, light and heavy at the same time.

"Maybe you're right."

I was afraid that perhaps some other student had decided to use the place as their sanctuary. What if they saw me? And her. I didn't want them to know. About us.

Her words reassured me a little, but something that day made me question my sanity instead.

I had been engrossed in the work before me that I failed to realize that the sun had started to set. Only when my shadow over the canvas began to shrink that I noticed how much time had passed.

I hurriedly put my palette and the brush on the table, intending to wipe it afterwards. I took off my apron and hung it on a nail by the window. I picked up a rag and went to the table, only to find the brush missing.

I looked over at the table, lifting some papers at the end to see if it had rolled underneath the pile. Nothing. I went down on my knees, scanning the floor. I found it by the doorway. It had fallen, but the window was closed.

I walked over and bent down to pick it up. I paused. Something was different about it. I picked it up and frowned. It was clean.

Hurriedly, I picked up my things and walked towards the door. Before leaving, I looked back at her as a way of saying goodbye. Strange. She looked as if she was smiling at me.

That image was burned into my mind even as I lay in my bed. I closed my eyes.

I felt something like a cold wind blowing into my neck. I shivered. It was only a little, and it stopped. On and off, as if someone was breathing into my neck.

"Sigh."

My eyes flew open. In the dark, lying beside me, was she - her expression was as it always was, cold and stiff. But her lips parted and closed, cold air escaping them as her empty eyes stared at me.

I jerked back, shocked. I fell to the floor with a loud thud. I opened my eyes and saw the morning light brightly flooding the windows. I was alone.

What did that mean? Was it an effect of my visits? Indeed, my visits became so frequent. My mind was so filled with her that maybe...

I tried to avoid going there. Maybe it was unhealthy for me. But as my classes reached the end, I found myself restless. I needed to go back. I needed to see her. What if the next time I return, she would be gone? Lost to me forever.

My legs brought me back to the old building. I ran into the room and found her there, in the very same spot. No, not the same spot. Was she closer to the window now?

A suspicion grew in my mind. I almost leaped in front of her. I grabbed her shoulders. She was stiff and cold. What was I thinking? She was not alive. I breathed a sigh of relief. She was as she always was and should be. I placed my head on her bosom, relishing the silence that we shared.

Once again, my work consumed me. I was filled with so much inspiration that by the time I set down my brush, the sun had already disappeared into the horizon.

"Thump."

What was that sound? I spun around. Did her eyes just blink? No, no. That's impossible. Outside, the crickets chirped loudly and the strong wind rustled the leaves of the surrounding trees. It was almost as if there were whispers. Whispers calling my name.

But it wasn't the wind. I scrambled out of the building. That night I couldn't sleep.

Was she alive? Perhaps… Was she calling out to me? I ran. But I shouldn't have. My intense love for her has given her life. I knew it. What else could it be?

For the first time, I visited the room before classes even started. I looked into her eyes.

"I love you too. I know it is wrong to act on my feelings, but I cannot help it anymore. A miracle has come forth because of my love."

I cupped her cheeks with my hands and did what I never dared to do. Place my lips on hers.

They were hard and cold and rough, and they made my heart leap with joy. I felt a sharp pain and tasted blood when her lips cracked under mine.

Her lips broke, then the crack traveled up to her nose to her forehead. I jumped back as the plaster broke into shards and… she gasped.

Life filled her lungs and her plaster-covered pupils met my gaze.

"My love…"

She stared at me. "You, you! What have you done?!" She screamed.

"I'm sorry. It's wrong of me, but I just love you so much."

"I don't love you. I can never love you!"

Joy was replaced with anger and my face clouded over with rage. How…I had brought her to life and how could she…

"I'm leaving." I grabbed the mallet and swung it over her head. Over and over again, I pounded.

I stood up, looking down on the shattered figure, plaster scattered everywhere as it floated on scarlet blood. Once more, she was dead.

"Gasp!"

I turned around to find my classmate gaping at me, her beautiful face ashen. Almost like… a statue. I swung my mallet.

I sat down and started to sketch. As always, she was beautiful. Her large eyes had long lashes and she had a sharp nose, and her figure was tall and buxom.

Ah, how could I dare love someone I can never touch?

ABOUT THE AUTHOR

Lizzette Adele Ardeña

"Addie" is a freelance content writer based in the Philippines. She works on articles and short story assignments after finishing work at her primary workplace. When it comes to writing, she enjoys horror the most.

Since starting freelance writing in 2017, she has delivered short stories, eBooks, and interactive fiction scripts in various genres. Horror and thriller are her most predominant works.

In her free time, she crochets children's clothes while watching horror movies or listening to podcasts about serial killers. Addie loves potatoes and dairy products.

She currently lives with her family, including three dogs and a cat.

STORY 8

The Crone Pit

Everywhere she looked, Reba saw evergreen trees, trees, and only trees. They had been driving along the mountain road for at least two hours now; to say the view was getting kinda old would be an understatement.

Jamie caught a glimpse of her sighing while he drove, he took her hand in his, "Hey, penny for your thoughts?" asked Jamie.

Reba sighed some more and said, "The trees Jamie, they all look the same."

Jamie chuckled, "I'm no tree expert, but I think if you looked closer you'll see that they're all actually different trees, you know, wildlife diversity and whatnot. If they were the same, they'd call this place a plantation and not a nature reserve."

"Fair enough," snorts Reba as she looked back out the window, more intently this time. Jamie's right, if you look closely, the trees do all look different, even when they're clearly the same species, they do have different leaves, different stems and---

---SUDDENLY Jamie stepped hard on the brakes. A deer had narrowly escaped them; they stared at its hind legs disappearing out into the darkness of the wood.

"What was that about nature being good for us?" asked Reba while Jamie continued to drive.

"Come on Reba, give it a rest will ya? You haven't been the same since your mom died; you're so stressed out your hair's falling off! I'm doing this for your own good for Christ's sake. Just chill, take the time to breathe, and appreciate it."

Reba sank into her chair and sighed, again, "Whatever you say…,"

Jamie rolled his eye and turned the radio on, a cheerful pop song played for him to sing along to, he was drumming his steering wheel all the way up the winding mountain road, trying his best to drown out Reba's negativity.

The cabin was exactly what you'd expect from such a place. Small, slightly dilapidated, and dusty but once Jamie got the fire going; you wouldn't find anywhere cozier than this. But of course, Reba just couldn't settle. She kept pacing around, dusting and cleaning every inch of the place, all while he reclined on the couch reading his kindle.

"I think I'll go for a walk," said Reba once she'd made sure the cabin was spotless.

Jamie briefly looked up from his eBook, the glow had cast a strange light over his face, "Sure, just don't wander off too far," he pointed out the window, it was sunny, "Might not look like it, but it gets dark quickly out here," Reba nodded and fetched her coat.

The woods felt like that one Robert Frost poem they made you read in primary school, "How did it go?" wondered Reba as she hiked. "The woods were lovely, dark and deep, but I have promises to keep, and-"

A doe stared at her; it was so close Reba swore that if she were to extend her hand, she would be able to pet it. But it stepped back and walked away from her with a limp, "Oh no, no, no! Did we do that to you?" asked Reba with pity in her eyes, "Wait! I can help! Wait!"

Reba chased after it, somehow the deer had made it a few feet away despite its limp, she started to catch up to it, when---

---She fell in! Straight down a narrow pit!

Mud and roots buried her under until she took a deep breath. She emerged like the undead. Reba spewed the dirt back out and panicked; she struggled to set herself free from all the mud.

No matter how hard she brushed them off, it clung to her and it was all over! She hated this! It was dirty and it was all over her, sticking to her, getting into her orifices! She could've swore she felt the mud going into the crevices of her nails, into her ear canals, it might just seep right into her pores!

Reba closed her eyes and continued reciting, this might just work, this might just keep her mind off of the dirt, "The woods are lovely, dark and deep, but I have promises to keep, and miles to go before I sleep, and miles to go before I sleep. And miles," Reba heaved, it worked, she was finally calm enough to take in her surroundings.

The drop was at least ten feet down, and she was in a cave with walls made of roots and bark. There was barely any light past the hole she fell into; she couldn't make out where the cave ended.

Reba immediately tried to climb up the roots, but they were too fragile for her to step on them for long. After every two steps up, she'd fall down to the bottom of the pit over and over again, right back where she started.

She understood that Jamie wouldn't be worrying about her just yet. Her watch showed that it would be another hour or so before it got dark. Her phone, that darned thing, also conveniently had zero bars right when she needed it most.

Reba had no other option but to lean against the roots and wait. She brought her knees in, held them close, kept herself balled up, and as warm as she possibly could in the damp cave.

Jamie will come looking for her soon, she knew he will. He'll find her and bring her home. He has to. Reba continued reciting the poem to keep her anxiety at bay, "The woods are lovely, dark and deep, but I have promises to keep, and miles to go before I sleep. The woods are lovely, dark and deep, but---"

"There are secrets I cannot keep..." said a croaky voice from the darkness.

"WHO'S THERE!" shouted Reba.

"The woods are lovely... dark and deep... but there are secrets I cannot keep... and miles to go before I sleep..." replied the voice.

"Who's there? I'm not afraid of you!"

"There are secrets I cannot keep!" shouted the voice back.

Using her phone as a flashlight, Reba stepped forward and found herself looking at an old woman with patchy white hair. She was curled up into a ball just like Reba was moments ago. The tree roots had grown around her ankles and wrists, fashioned as a sort of chain that kept her in place. The old woman looked up, and Reba saw directly into milky white eyes.

The woman bared her rotten teeth, flashing a crooked smile, "There's secrets I cannot keep girl! And now I'll finally get to tell them!" she screamed to Reba's face. Reba was taken aback; she fell onto the cave floor. Staring out in horror at the old woman.

"Stay away! Stay back!" but Reba saw her recoil, curl back up into a ball on the floor, so she said softly, "My fiancé will be here soon and he'll help us both."

The old woman snarled, "But he won't come can't you see?

"What do you mean!?"

"Jamie won't come around Reba, he'll leave you here…to rot!" hissed the old woman.

Reba stepped forward again, she shined the light directly at the woman's face, stinging her eyes and backing her off to the cave wall,

"What the fuck did you just say!?" screamed Reba. The old woman; the Crone, started to laugh. It was shrill and high pitched. How you'd imagine a witch's laugh to be.

"I'm what you will become Reba! Look at me, take a good look at me! It's been decades and I'm still stuck here in this godforsaken hole! Jamie's left! And he never looked back!"

And Reba did take a good look at her. To her horror, she noticed the old woman was wearing the exact same coat she had on, only it had been tattered, worn out from age and the elements. Could it really be? That face… it looked just like her mother's before she died.

"I'm you! And let me tell you girl! NO ONE! Absolutely no one is coming to get you! You'll be forgotten and he will move on! He'll marry a normal girl, one that isn't so fucked up in her head! She'll make sweet love to him day and night, and they'll have kids, and a normal house with a white picket fence, the kind of life that you will never have! And you! YOU! You will be left here and forgotten!"

Reba sat on the floor and took her words in. She stared out into the distance. In the darkness, the cave of roots seemed to go on and on forever, an endless tunnel.

"I'm definitely hallucinating, but if you're me, at least tell me this, why did we decide to stay here and rot?" she shined her flashlight down the cave, "This tunnel... it must lead somewhere..."

The Crone laughed out loud again, "Why don't you try and find out girl?" The Crone smiled, it was a smile that held secrets indeed, Reba had a feeling she knew exactly what awaited down the tunnel and it didn't seem like anything good, she retreated back to where she first dropped and sat down.

This was still her best chance if she wanted ever make it out again. Jamie will certainly come for her. No matter what the Crone said. The Crone who sat there and stared daggers at her, eyes like a predator waiting to pounce at any given moment if not for her chain of roots.

"HEEEELP!" screamed Reba. She continued screaming until her throat was coarse and dry. She coughed out. A bottle of water would feel like heaven right now, but there was nothing but dirty puddles of rain water, Reba slumped, she closed her eyes and continued reciting the poem like a prayer.

"The woods are lovely, dark and deep, But I have promises to keep..."

"SECRETS I CANNOT KEEP!" shouted the Crone.

Reba continued to recite her poem; she started to cry and said out loud, "Promises! I promised my mother I'd live my life, no matter what, even if Jamie doesn't come to get me, I can't just throw my life away!" The Crone went silent.

After what felt like forever, it started to rain. The droplets were welcomed refreshment; she cupped her hands and took sips. Reba didn't mind how dirty it was, she just clung to the hope that it will help get her voice back. It'll mean she'll be able to scream again, and Jamie will hear exactly where she was and come running for her.

"HEEEEELP!" shouted Reba helplessly, yet no one replied. If anything, the rain started to pick up its pace. The water rose to her ankles.

"How is this possible?" she thought, "Guess the cave isn't endless after all. Good, then we'll be able to swim out of this hell hole."

Reba stood up when the water reached her knee, she wobbled over to The Crone who sat motionless against the roots, worried, despite everything she said, that she might have drowned. But at the slosh of her footsteps, The Crone turned to look at her with those eerie white eyes again. "Leave me be girl!" she chastised.

"No! We can swim our way out of here! The water will keep on rising and it'll make it easier for us to get out!"

The Crone snarled, "Can't you see I'm shackled to where I am?"

"Then I'll help you break free! They're roots, trees, not iron for Christ's sake!" said Reba as she reached the Crone.

A torrent of water came in then, the water level it reached her neck, the Crone was completely submerged. Reba took a deep breath and dove underwater, she tried to pull at the roots but they didn't budge.

The Crone head butted her, she stared at her with those milky white eyes, every inch of her telling her to go, and she mouthed those exact words, "Go! Now!" and The Crone let out a few air bubbles. She went completely still.

Reba tried and tried to break the roots off, it was futile, she held on to dear life, running on the very last reserve of her breath. Then she let go.

There was a current in the pit and it dragged her down the tunnel. Reba swam up, gasping for air, she realized the current took her deeper into the tunnel while also taking her around in circles.

It was a large doughnut shaped space. Time and time again, she'd pass by the hole she slipped into. She would try to no avail to reach it, to free herself from this cursed pit. The currents were always too strong and she was already too weak to hold on to anything by the hole. Nothing there helped her.

"HEEEELP!" she screamed, clinging on to the last bit of hope that Jamie might just hear her, that he'll take her hand in his and pull her up. No such thing happened. Reba just kept floating round and round in circles, helplessly thrown around by the currents. She gave up and closed her eyes, hoping to drown just like the old Crone.

Reba woke up at the bottom of the pit, covered head-to-toe in mud. She felt weak, too weak to do anything. So she just laid there and closed her eyes.

Eventually the roots grew around her ankles and wrists, fusing her with the cave. She had nowhere to go and no one came for her. She could no longer tell day from night, or how long had it been since she first fell into the pit, perhaps it had been five hours or perhaps it had been fifty years.

But then she heard it, just a few meters away, the voice of a young girl reciting a poem, but she was reciting it wrong.

"The woods are lovely, dark and deep, but I have promises to keep, and miles to go before I sleep...The woods are lovely, dark and deep, but-"

"There are secrets I cannot keep..." Reba said out loud.

It had been eons since she'd last spoken, and what came out was the croaky voice of an old woman.

ABOUT THE AUTHOR

Pia Diamandis

Pia Diamandis, (Jakarta, 1999) is a horror screen and fiction writer who sometimes doubles as an art curator. After finishing her Art History studies in Istituto Marangoni Firenze, she now works as assistant to horror/action film director, TimoTjahjanto - https://mubi.com/cast/timo-tjahjanto

From time to time, she will write film & art columns for online media like Tirto.id - https://tirto.id/author/piadiamandisutm_source=tirtoid&utm_medium =lowauthor and the Gen-Z culture collective, Broadly Specific - https://broadly-specific.com/author/piadiamandis/

She has co-curated an exhibition for Museo Salvatore Ferragamo (2022), performed as assistant curator for the Forme Nel Verde - https://www.formenelverde.com/ outdoor sculpture festival (2018), and worked as a consultant for state museums in Jakarta (2019 - 2021).

While in terms of scary things, she enjoys all things gore and creature horror, particularly those rooted in local lores that are set in current times.

You can find her on instagram @pia_diamandis

Or check out her full portfolio at https://linktr.ee/Pia_diamandis

STORY 9

The Tortured Artist

My name is Margene, and I am only 26. Most people who see my name on a form assume that they are about to meet a woman in her 60s. I like to think of it as my parents' most fucked-up prank.

Growing up in the 90s was tough with a grandma's name. It was like always being a nobody next to names like Victoria and her posse of Jessicas and Natalies. They weren't your average bullies; they were stealthy.

Victoria never paraded her popularity around; she befriended everyone and was seen as a humanitarian to most. That's what made her so sadistic- how in the shadows, she could slither around, evading anyone from ever seeing her true form. Why did she choose me? Jealousy.

Victoria tortured me behind the scenes for being who I was on life's stage. I had a lot of feelings and saw the world in a unique way. She couldn't stand that she wouldn't experience the type of passion I feel when I am making an art piece. I would pour my heart and soul into an art piece at school, only to find the next day that it was smashed or retransfigured into a penis.

She kept me in the dark for a long time. I had no clue who was ruining my art, but when they did, a piece of me died with it. You see, I don't believe that art can be recreated. When I create a piece, I feel ecstasy, and ecstasy never feels the same way twice.

Why would I remake something that is a watered-down version of the original? Recreating it was never an option for me. I spent many nights in college mourning the loss of an expressed memory.

The professor told me to keep my art at home until we find out who is responsible. I thought it was unfair for me to have to do so. One night I finally decided to hide in the art room and wait to see who it was.

When I saw Victoria, trailed by her Jessicas and Natalies, I couldn't help but burst out from hiding, screaming like a lunatic. "What are you doing!?" I squealed out as I jumped down from my hiding spot in the cabinet. I think her posse all pissed themselves. I'm sure I looked like proof that vampires exist, but Victoria didn't even quiver.

She actually laughed, then proceeded to bring my clay sculpture of the beautiful Kauri trees of New Zealand and smash it in my face.

Kauri trees are known for their strength, and I made sure my sculpture was proportionate to their magnitude. It broke my nose and knocked my front teeth loose. I started screaming at the sight of blood trickling down my shirt, but by the time I looked up, Victoria was dumping a glaze bucket over my head.

I remember everything moving in slow motion. The confusion made it all so fuzzy. The torture after that night increased. My soul no longer only died with my art pieces, but it died every day in the hallways, and every night I tossed and turned in bed. I would have dropped out after Victoria's last prank if I could even remember it. I'm still trying to wash out the hot candle wax from when she tried to mold my head when I had fallen asleep in class.

I woke up to my skin melting off the left side of my face. I stood up in a panic, screeching from the pain. Classmates all staring at me with horrified eyes as I stumbled and crashed into desks. Papers flew all around me as I grasped my face, howling like a werewolf in heat.

I felt my head hit the side of the potter's wheel, there was a loud crack, and then I woke up in the hospital three months later with no memory.

I would see Victoria and her posse's families around campus often, as they were alumni. Their parents liked me a lot and said I had true potential. I was apparently close to Victoria's mom, Ms. Jones. She took a special interest in ensuring my success.

But when she came to see me after I woke up, I couldn't remember who she was. Ms. Jones spent hours in my hospital room, showing me photos of old work I had done, telling me memories of contests I've won, and showing me all the colleges that wanted to give me full ride scholarships if my final project got an A grade.

I remembered some things, others were fuzzy, or just not in my memory. She would come once a week to show me the photos of my old art projects. I think she hoped for me to get my memory back more than I did.

About two months into her visits, I finally remembered one of my art pieces, the sculpture of the Kauri trees. Once my memory unlocked, I couldn't keep my eyes off it. Ms. Jones let me keep the photo and promised to return next week.

I started getting impatient with my healing process. My face was scarred over by now, so I started demanding that the nurses release me. I didn't feel pain anymore and remembered all the important stuff.

There was no reason for me to still be there. The doctor finally made a deal that when Ms. Jones returned, he would discuss my leaving. I took the deal.

I started doing art in my hospital room; just painting as working with clay would make it unsanitary. Don't get me wrong, I loved painting, but nothing felt as good as when I felt my heart pour into my hands and out my fingertips to capture the essence of something wonderful.

I itched for it, so I painted the Kauri trees again and again, and the whole room became lined with them, each one from a different angle and perspective. My room looked like a movie set trying to imitate New Zealand's land.

As I was finishing the largest painting of the Kauri tree, Ms. Jones showed up. I called for the doctor, and he came in, not even giving Ms. Jones a second glance. He immediately started explaining that I was being held under psychiatric watch as I was a danger to myself and others.

He retold the story of what had happened to bring me there, of a girl jumping up in the middle of class for no reason, screeching like a wild beast while flipping tables, and then tripping and knocking herself out on a clay wheel. The story made my head hurt, my stomach twisted in knots, and it just felt wrong inside me.

Though my memory was shot at the moment, my artist spirit was alive and feeling things fiercely. He continued on using serious words like "schizophrenic" and "hallucinations." Then he held a mirror in front of my face to reveal there were no scars on my face. Why did I think I had scars? He said schizophrenia could be triggered by stress or trauma.

After months of therapy, I was finally released. I started working on my scholarship art piece, which was going to be displayed at my art show. It took a couple of weeks to get back into sculpting, but eventually, my hands remembered what to do and the art started to flow again.

Even though I still couldn't remember much, I had learned techniques to reduce my reaction to stressful situations. I religiously practiced these techniques, and they kept my schizophrenia episodes at bay. Besides Ms. Jones, I didn't have many friends. Her daughter visited me often, and while she was nice, I always felt a little uneasy around her.

However, I enjoyed sharing my art with her, and she seemed genuinely interested in why I was creating a Kauri forest for my final piece. We both struggled to understand why that was the only art piece I could remember. I thought it was just out of curiosity until the day before my big art show when she strongly urged me to choose a different subject for my piece.

She wanted me to come up with a new concept and execute it in 12 hours. I felt protective of my art, and my blood boiled as I could feel my anger rising. She was panicking and speaking in a way that made it seem like dark clouds were coming out of her mouth.

She begged for forgiveness and said she wanted to be absolved of her guilt. My brain tingled, and I felt like there was a crack in my skull as my mind retraced every moment of the last four years. "Say something, please! I need you to forgive me. I didn't mean to do this to you," Victoria sobbed.

All the pain and anger rushed through me. I remembered the Kauri trees, the countless times I bled at her hand, the laughter as I was mercilessly tortured. My fingers rubbed over the scars on my legs and arms, and I recalled the sharp pricks of the sewing needles she had placed in my seat cushion one day. My eyes turned dark, and I started to vibrate. Victoria started to slither on the ground like a serpent without a face.

I felt my body surge forward, grasping at its slithery neck. Victoria's body came back into view as I slid the sharp steel end of my molding tool directly into her belly button.

I'll never forget the crunch that flesh makes when you inflict trauma on it. I felt the skin spread apart up my whole arm. Victoria grasped my shoulders, her eyes wide with terror, her mouth gaping in a gasp, finally unable to spew more lies. I held her there until I eventually didn't see a body anymore.

The feral instincts took over, and I lost my fists in her belly as I smeared her steaming blood on the trunks of the Kauri trees. They reached to the ceiling, and their roots covered the floor completely.

The paintings I did in the hospital were lining the wall, the lighting a deep yellow so viewers could have a surreal moment with the power of these magical beings.

Vines were my newest addition, and I hung Victoria's intestines among the branches. I added clay and dry dirt; it mixed well with the deep red. "People will worship my artwork tonight," I said through my teeth as I tore further into her. Every tear and fluid squirt fueled my desire.

You wouldn't have known it was a body if it weren't for her

perfect legs still attached. I had let out four years of rage; her upper body was splayed open. It looked as if beasts had devoured an unsuspecting seal. After moments of catching my breath, I dragged her body to the back of my biggest Kauri and shoved her inside. No one would notice the blood on the floor because it blended in with the roots.

I spent all night molding and shaping this tree around Victoria. I let all my darkness out, and that's why I got the scholarship to continue my education.

No one seemed to like my art show more than Ms. Jones, though. It was as if her daughter was calling to her because she spent most of the night getting lost under the vines, dancing with the trunk of the tree as she downed another vodka soda. "I have never felt more free," is what she sang to me that night.

Everyone drank and danced to the ethereal electronic music I hand-selected to trigger different parts of my viewers' brains. I danced too.

I danced with everyone, and everyone danced with me. I felt an ecstasy I would forever be chasing to feel again. My body swayed until my feet melded into the roots, and then my legs, pelvis, chest, until finally, my whole body became one with my forest.

And everyone dancing within it became a part of it.

ABOUT THE AUTHOR

Stephanie Bojanek

Greetings, dear reader! My name is Stephanie, and I am a lifelong writer. From the moment I was able to hold a pen, I have been in love with the written word. I have spent countless hours pouring my thoughts and feelings onto the page, exploring new ideas and expressing myself in ways that only writing can capture.

As I grew older, my love for writing only grew stronger. I read every book I could get my hands on, studying the greats and learning from their mastery of the craft. I honed my skills through practice, constantly challenging myself to improve and push beyond my limits.

And now, as an adult, I am proud to say that I am a professional writer. I have had the opportunity to share my writing with the world, to connect with readers who are touched by my words and inspired by my stories. Writing is more than just a passion for me - it is a calling, a purpose that I have dedicated my life to fulfilling.

Instagram: @bakedlbeans

Vocal: h ttps://vocal.media/authors/stephanie-bojanek

Youtube: https://www.youtube.com/channel/UCaHmz_dG-cF10uSWeZPY2UA

STORY 10

The Bridge

For all of those who have asked, I have very little to tell. All I can only say for certain is that it was something dark. A hunched, huddled shape, something like a shadow, glimpsed for just for an instant from the corner of my eye.

It stayed for a moment, like a smudge or an inky blur, on the very edge of vision, before, in a flash of thick black hair, it disappeared again. Back beneath the bridge.

There were three of us there that day. Just like always. From the moment we'd met in a registration class on the first day of high school, right up to the day that he went missing, Dale and I along with our mutual friend Robbie had been virtually inseparable.

To cut a long story short, any place you found one of us, you were likely to find the other two trailing close behind. Though of course on the day it happened, close behind, was not close enough.

My Grandad used to call us the Three Musketeers, after the novel by Alexandre Dumas. We used to laugh about this, especially since we had only heard of the three musketeers from a kids cartoon show called 'Dogtanian' but I will admit that sometimes, when we were careening around the park on our BMXs, building dens in the local woods or seeing off bullies by sticking together, we kinda did think of ourselves in that way.

Three best friends in a tight little gang of heroes, 'all for one and one for all'. Problem is, if you have a gang of heroes you're going to need a villain and what the cartoons and books don't tell you, is that sometimes, the bad guys win.

We had all heard the stories of course. The twice told tales, fables and folktales that somehow crept into every playground, like weeds grasping up through the cracks in the concrete. Wherever you went, they were there, whispered in corners, at torch lit sleepovers or in the steamy damp of the school cloakrooms during some sodden, break-time huddle. Somewhere along the line you were bound to hear them.

Those urban legends and modern myths were told as if they were true. Terrible things that the teller swore had happened to 'a friend of a friend'. They all had the same pattern these stories and were you able to tear them apart and look at them, piece by piece, you'd probably find they were made up of the same ingredients.

Half heard truths and pockets of rumor, warped by lies and exaggeration, stitched together with the clumsy fumbling of teenage hands and mixed with a snatch of ragged fragments, torn from films and fairytales to form a hideous, patchwork narrative. A story made from a mash of others that felt like something new.

Of all the stories told at our school however, it was not a new one that stood out above all, but the oldest. The one about, The Bridge in the Clough and the thing that lived beneath it.

Even amongst the jostling crowd of hooked handed men and crocs in the sewers, this story stood out. Partly because it concerned a place we all knew and partly because of its age.

You see, this story did not start with us and our friends, but with our parents and their parents before them. It was an old story, told to kids in our town for generations, repeated, not only at schools and sleepovers, but also by successive generations of parents, all trying to ensure that their kids would obey and be sure to be back by curfew. Looking back now, I often think it was this last element that made the story stick for us and what made it far more terrifying.

You see, with other monsters it is easy to point and laugh. Whilst the creatures on the movie screen might scare you at the time, afterwards you can smile. Safe in the knowledge that the monsters aren't real.

"They're Just men in costumes" your folks would say "actors wearing makeup". It's safe to laugh at them, because they are make-believe. With the thing beneath the bridge though, it was different. With him, your fears were never dismissed. Instead they were confirmed. He wasn't make-believe or an actor wearing makeup. Like all the best bogeymen, the power of this creature came from the fact that your parents sanctioned it. This monster, they told you, was real.

When they told you as a child that you had to get across that bridge and out of the park by sundown. Told you that if you didn't, if you were just one minute late, then the thing that lived beneath would take you away and eat you, they said it as a warning, but also like they meant it.

Whereas at night they'd tell you there were no such things as ghosts, that monsters aren't real and that to believe in them was silly, when it came to that bridge, it didn't seem so silly. He was the exception because he, they said, was real.

Of course looking back, I realize that there was a reason for this. The Thing Beneath the Bridge was meant as a deterrent. The story, that if you entered via the bridge you had to leave by it and be out by sundown, was a convenient way of making sure that any kids, venturing into the park via the bridge in the morning, were safely back across it and on their way home by the time the twilight came.

The Thing beneath the Bridge, like some troll in Billy Goat's Gruff, was a spook story, meant to protect the kids from the very real dangers of being in the park at night.

A bogeyman meant to scare us straight. I'm sure they assumed that by the time we hit puberty we'd have forgotten all about the thing beneath the bridge and would just come home, because we knew we had a curfew.

What they didn't realize, was just how deep that cut had gone. How that story, reinforced every day when we sprinted or pedalled as fast as we could to get across and away, stayed with us all and lingered. Biding its time and waiting for the right moment to bite.

What our parents couldn't have foreseen, was how that threat, the promise that if you were not back across that bridge by the time the sun went down, you would soon be devoured, became a kind of game. A stupid teenage dare of the kind young boys always love.

Even as adolescents, aged sixteen and cocky as hell, we still played up to the myth. Pretending to each other that we still believed or least pretending to pretend. Pretending or not we always ensured we were back on time.

The bridge itself was the one of two entrances into the park we referred to as the Clough, a wooded area close to where we lived that had been a recreational space for kids and families for generations.

It was made from stone, was slightly arched in the middle and spanned the small valley that led down to the stream separating the park gates from the main wooded area. The idea in our game was to cross it in the morning, spend the day riding around in the woods and then when the time came, dare each other to stay for as long as you possibly could on the wrong side of the bridge.

After crossing the bridge with no problem earlier in the day to access the park, we would hang around till the clouds began to turn pink. Silently egging each other on to stay longer and longer. There was no question of any of us remaining until after sunset. Not only because of the threat of the 'Thing' but because being in the park after dark was not a good idea. Not to mention a grounding offence.

So, as the sun began to slowly descend, we'd jump on our bikes and race, hurtling as fast as we could down the hill that led to the bridge in a desperate attempt not to be last to cross it. The idea wasn't to just stay in the park, but to get across to safety before sundown whilst cutting it as close as possible, getting across with only seconds to spare. That was the adventure.

Whether any of us really believed in the possible consequences of not making it across wasn't important. The point was that we all pretended it was real. Accepting at face value the idea that if we didn't make it across, we were done for. An idea made all the more potent by real life events.

In the five years that I attended the local high school, at least eight people, four of them kids from that very same school, vanished without a trace in our town. Three were adults. A pensioner named Jim Gross, who was a regular at the pub my dad drank in, Majorie White, a young teacher at one of the local primary schools and Andy Turnton a young lad in his early twenties who was supposed to be going off to University, but instead disappeared into thin air.

Of course there could be logical explanations for all of these cases and even for the kids. They might have run away, been kidnapped or been the victims of some kind of nasty accident. In the folklore of the playground however, there was only one explanation.

All of them had ventured out into the Clough and had all come back too late. In our retellings they had wandered back just as the sun went down and had heard somewhere behind them a faint scratching sound, or perhaps the sound of hooves, clacking the stone behind them. Then, they were gone. Dragged below by taloned hands, by a thing, covered in wiry hair, that would rip and chew through flesh, as it cracked and ground the bones.

That was why, we'd say, no trace was ever found. No clues for police to hunt, no trail of evidence. They had all come back too late, had all gone beneath and had all been devoured.

The day Dale disappeared, he vanished without a trace. Not here today, gone tomorrow, but vanished, in an instant like a cheap magician's trick. One second he was there, then suddenly he wasn't. You see, in real life, it isn't like the movies, where the monster crashes with a deafening bang or stalks its prey as violins stab and slash behind. In real life, when a predator comes to claim its prey, when evil reaches hungrily up to snatch with taloned hands, it does so very quickly and in almost total silence.

We had raced, as we had every day for years, down the hill and round the bend, freewheeling over the bridge and up the other side, panting through a mix of laughter and jeers and were pedalling ever homeward. Only this time, it was different. This time we waited too long. As Robbie and I streamed up the opposite bank, shouting and hollering for Dale to come, but never stopping to even look back, the air around us changed.

Maybe it was the cold. The icy, electric crackle of a chill Autumn night, or perhaps the fact that just this once, we'd allowed the sun to sink and the dark to pool around us, but something, something was different.

It was Robbie who pulled up first. Talking about it later he said he didn't know why. Perhaps he had noticed, even if not consciously, that our three voices had somehow turned to two. Perhaps he was used to Dale taking the lead or preferred to be at the back, but for whatever reason he slammed on his brakes so that I had to swerve and narrowly avoid him.

Before I could collect myself and bawl at him for stopping, he was already looking back behind me. Calling Dale's name and not getting no answer.

I remember dropping my bike, turning back toward the bridge and expecting to find Dale, streaming back across it with a stupid smirk across his face, knowing that he'd killed the myth once and for all. Instead, I saw nothing. Just the bridge, stony and solid. On top, a space that looked not so much empty as vacant. As if only moments before, someone or something had occupied that space, but was now conspicuously gone.

Robbie and I looked at each other and swallowed hard. I called Dale again. But rather than a voice, only the rustle of half dried leaves rose up to greet me, I waited. Allowing the silence to bleed out and grow as the sky above grew darker and darker.

Eventually I told Robbie that we would have to go back. To check and see where Dale had gone. 'In case' I remember saying, 'he's fallen in the stream. Slipped off his bike and cracked his head'. Robbie, though, refused to move. Instead, he simply stood there, gently shaking his head. Stubborn, obstinate and terrified. I left my bike where it was.

Slowly, cautiously, I made my way back down the hill and toward the bridge. I remember clearly how all around me the too sweet smell of rotting leaves, of moistened soil and dampened wood rose up to meet me. As if that one sense were trying to fill the gap, to compensate somehow, for the sudden stop in another. For all I heard, was silence.

Still, I listened. Calling out for Dale, I glanced back at Robbie, who was still rooted, firm to the spot and still shaking his head. Then the sound came.

I have tried many times to convince myself that sound was a breaking branch. A twig snapped under foot as Dale ran away, or some other animal scurried from my path. I have tried many times, but many times I've failed. The sound that came was not a branch, but a low wet snap, followed by a strange liquid ripping, that I hate to recall and hate even more to imagine the cause of. It was then, looking toward the other bank, that I saw something move.

To this day I know that if I was given a pen and paper and asked to draw what I'd seen, the image would not be clear. So fast and so indistinct was that flash of something, that I still find it hard even to describe it. Yet I have not a single grain of doubt, that there was something there and that the something wasn't Dale.

I ran. Turned back toward Robbie, jumped on my bike and peddled away faster than I ever had in my life. Back at home, I screamed to my parents almost in tears that the thing beneath the bridge had gotten Dale. At first they tried to laugh it off, as I was trying some kind of prank. Soon enough though they saw that I was serious and I watched their faces drop. It was at that moment I realized, they were frightened too. Saw that their own parents had scarred them with stories. Had told them, when they were young, that the thing beneath the bridge, was as dangerous as it was real.

Despite his fear, my father, alongside Dale's parents and a few others, went down to the Clough. Torch in hand, he descended the bank on the entrance side of the bridge and scrambled down toward the stream. He did not find Dale or even his bike, but he did come back with a look on his face that will haunt me for the rest of my life.

I never saw Dale again and within six months of his disappearance both Robbie's family and my own had moved away from the area.

Around a year ago, shortly before he died, my father shared with me what he'd found beneath the bridge that day. It had been years, he said, but he remembered as if it was yesterday. What he'd seen, he told me quietly, were footprints. Larger and wider than any man's, barefooted and evenly spaced, trailing in the mud all along the bank.

They were, according to him "More like the prints of a bear or a dog" having as they did the marks of claws, at the end of every toe. Worse even than this however, was what he found beside the tracks. A long, thin, uneven streak. A trail or rut, carved through the mud, as if whatever had been walking here, had dragged something heavy beside it.

ABOUT THE AUTHOR

Eleanor Sciolistein

Eleanor Sciolistein is 37 and lives in Derbyshire, England with her two feline accomplices Pluto and Vert.

She is a writer and collector of poems, essays and stories.

Her favourite hobby is handwriting short stories into the flyleaves of books, before donating them to charity shops and thrift stores for unsuspecting customers to find and enjoy.

Thank you so much for purchasing my book!

If you have the time, it would help me a lot if you could leave a review or just rate my book.

Printed in Great Britain
by Amazon

43312169R00069